THE DINNER GUESTS

KIERSTEN MODGLIN

Cover Design by Kiersten Modglin
Copy Editing by Three Owls Editing
Proofreading by My Brother's Editor
Formatting by Kiersten Modglin

First Print and Electronic Edition: 2022
kierstenmodglinauthor.com

This one's to the people we used to be.
And to everyone striving to make their former self proud.

CHAPTER ONE

LAKYNN

The moving trucks came without warning. I was at the window that morning, sipping the steaming coffee in my mug, when I noticed them. There were three in total—all white with green logos on their sides.

They belonged to a company I'd never heard of, a rarity in our small town. After they'd parked the trucks around the curve of the cul-de-sac—one after the other in a neat row—men in matching green polos and black pants stepped out of the trucks. There were nine movers altogether, and they milled about for a moment, stretching their legs and laughing with each other about a joke I couldn't hear through the panes of glass.

My phone buzzed in the pocket of my robe, and I pulled it out, checking the screen.

"Hello?"

"Are you seeing this?" Bethany asked. Though I couldn't see my best friend through the curtains of the house across the street, I knew she was there, watching it all unfold the same as I was.

"Yeah. *Three* trucks?"

"It's a *big* house," she said simply. And she was right. The house at the end of our cul-de-sac was the largest on the street, triple the size of the next largest. All my life, it had been owned by the family who'd founded our subdivision, the Burnetts. Tom and Eleanor Burnett were an eccentric couple, several years older than us, and incredibly wealthy. Their house had been decorated so elaborately every Christmas, we'd had to put room-darkening curtains on our windows facing their home. The kids had loved it and we'd adjusted.

The Burnetts had the kind of wealth that allowed them to take month-long vacations several times a year, which was why we'd originally thought nothing of it when several months went by without us seeing them.

Then, one day just a few weeks ago, a set of local moving trucks arrived and hauled out Tom and Eleanor's things, and we knew they'd left for good. There one day and gone the next.

"I can't believe they're really not coming back," Bethany whispered somewhat nostalgically.

Though we'd never considered Eleanor and Tom friends, they were friendly enough. They'd been kind to us. We'd had neighborhood barbecues, holiday parties, and they'd brought us dinner when we'd had each of the kids. With Tom and Eleanor, we never worried about letting the kids play in the streets. This place—our home—felt safe.

But now...

A new neighbor brought so many unknowns.

For the last week, there had been no movement at the house whatsoever. It sat completely empty, its presence taunting us with unknowns. There'd never even been a For Sale sign in the yard.

Now, here was the proof that they truly had left.

That we hadn't imagined it.

And that someone new was coming.

"I wouldn't expect them to have made anything other than a dramatic exit," I said with a chuckle.

"I figured there'd be a parade," she agreed.

Finally, the movers began unloading the trucks, carrying bubble-wrapped furniture and long, rolled-up rugs by the armful into the house.

"Those look expensive," she said, watching as three men unloaded an oversized chaise lounge chair.

Before I could respond, I felt a pair of hands slip around my waist. Henry's head came to rest on my shoulder. I breathed in his scent—an inexplicable scent that could only be described as warmth. Safety. If I could bottle it, I would.

"What are you two gossiping about?" he asked, without having to question whom I might be talking to. He nudged the curtain aside, waving across the street, then spied the moving trucks. "Ah."

"Someone's moving in."

"Ooh, what've we got?" He chuckled, rubbing his hands together as he stepped away from me.

"Put me on speaker," Bethany ordered.

I did as she said before answering Henry. "So far just the movers."

He nodded, already losing interest.

"Mom wants to know if you liked that kimchi, Henry?" Bethany said, speaking louder than necessary.

He chuckled. "Is she over there?"

"Mhm."

He grinned with one corner of his mouth. "You tell Ms. Siu that I love everything she's ever brought me, but that might've been my favorite."

Bethany repeated the message in Korean. I only ever heard her speaking Korean when talking to her parents or when she was especially angry.

Henry pointed a thumb over his shoulder. "I'm running to town. Do you need anything?"

"We're out of iced coffee. And Aaron needs more face wash."

"Got it," he said. "Bye, Beth."

"Bye," she called over the speaker, then cleared her throat. "Oh, looks like Piper's coming over."

I checked out the window to my left, spying my neighbor crossing her front yard on her way into mine.

"She looks upset. Let me see what's going on. Want me to call you back?"

"I'm coming over, too," she said, ending the call instantly.

I heard the garage door opening, its dull roar echoing through the house, and watched Henry back out of the drive as Piper stepped onto the porch. I reached the door before she could knock, and swung it open.

"Hey."

"Hey," she said, brows wiggling as she jutted her head toward the moving trucks. "Did you see?"

"Yeah, Beth and I were just talking about it." I pointed

behind her, to where Beth was jogging across the street dressed in loud-patterned workout gear.

I stepped back, letting them both inside, and shut the door. Together, the three of us moved back to the window.

"We probably look ridiculous," Piper whispered.

"They're not even paying attention," I assured her.

"What do you think they're like?" Beth asked.

"Maybe we could go over and introduce ourselves this evening. Or tomorrow. Bring over a Sunday dinner," Piper offered.

"Oh, good idea. Everyone loves a 'welcome to the neighborhood' casserole," Beth agreed.

"I just hope they're normal," I said softly.

"You mean like us right now?" Beth asked. We exchanged glances as Piper snorted, causing us all to laugh in spite of ourselves.

I closed the blinds before we made our way across the room, changing the subject. We'd go meet the new neighbors soon, and I was sure all my fears would be eased.

At least, that was what I thought.

After all, no one ever expects their neighbors will try to kill them.

CHAPTER TWO

BETHANY

W e didn't introduce ourselves that evening, nor any evening that followed. Over the next few days, unfamiliar vans and loud equipment trucks filled our usually quiet subdivision.

Security companies, too—men dressed all in black coming and going with earpieces and grim expressions. They installed cameras to cover every square inch of the home's exterior, and based on the equipment I'd seen being hauled inside, I assumed the home was more secure than a maximum-security prison.

Celebrities didn't live in Poe.

It was too small, hours from the nearest city, without access to an airport, and despite being a cute little town, there was nothing particularly interesting about it.

Even knowing all of that, I couldn't help wondering who our new neighbor might be. Perhaps it was just someone with a lot of money. That, at least, wasn't unheard of, albeit rare, in our town. Or maybe it was a business owner. Maybe a criminal. An escaped prisoner. A drug lord. Whatever curiosity I'd had originally was growing to feel more like fear every day.

What if the new neighbor turned our quiet street into a heavily trafficked area, bringing with him all sorts of shady characters?

Blair Lane was my home.

It was where all three of my children had grown up.

It was where so many of my memories had been made.

I had no desire to leave this place, but what if I had to now? What if I had no choice? And how quickly would property values drop if bad things started happening here? We'd practically have to give the house away.

And, if we did that, how would we buy anything comparable? You couldn't find anything for the price we'd paid for our home twenty years ago. And we were paying for Noelle's college tuition. Jacob had just turned sixteen and would be expecting a car. How was I going to tell them we were going to lose everything?

I steadied myself against the door to an exam room.

My next patient was waiting for me.

I needed to focus.

I didn't have time to spiral. Not when my entire dental practice was counting on me to steer the ship.

I tried to keep myself busy, to keep my mind from wandering—between work and three kids, it wasn't exactly hard—but over the next few weeks, I found myself growing more and more paranoid.

Something wasn't right about our new neighbor.

It had been so long since I'd felt worried like this. The painful kind that sets into your bones, making every inch of your body light up with electricity at the slightest sound or disturbance. The swooping panic that courses through you as possibilities swim through your head, each one worse than the last.

I couldn't tell my friends, though.

I could tell them almost everything, but I couldn't tell them this. Not if I wanted—needed—them to believe I was still as strong as I'd once been.

CHAPTER THREE

PIPER

A knock on the door interrupted my work, and I checked the time at the corner of my computer screen. I'd been known to get so wrapped up in my work that I wouldn't come up for air for hours at a time, so I was relieved to see it was just past noon.

I stood from my desk, stretching my arms above my head with a groan, and checked my reflection in the hall mirror as I made my way toward the door. Sunlight burned my eyes through the three large, identical windows on the far wall as I ran a hand through my hair, trying to coerce the shoulder-length blonde strands to life.

Accepting that there was no use, I approached the door. As I did, I began to make out the outline of his shadow through the frosted pane of glass in the center. At the sight, blood pounded in my ears. I wished I'd taken longer to check my appearance.

I sucked in a deep breath and reached for the door, swinging it open with a forced confidence.

"Hey!" *No.* I'd meant to come off casual, but even to my own ears, it was too loud. Too cheerful.

The scent of the lavender bushes near my porch hit me, and I breathed the calming scent in as if it were a life force. *Breathe, Piper.*

"Hey." Shane's smile warmed when he saw me, the wrinkles near his eyes deepening. "Sorry to bother you. I wanted to pay you back for the extra coffee the other morning." He held up a to-go bag from a local Italian place, wiggling it in the air. The scent of buttery garlic bread wafted toward me. "So, I brought you lunch." He paused, waiting for me to say something. Anything.

"Oh. Um, well, you didn't need to do that. I told you, the coffee was Allen's. It was lodged in the back of the cabinet, so you saved it from a fate of being wasted. I can't stand the taste of it." I waved off the gesture, leaning against the door in what I hoped looked like a carefree manner.

"I know. That's why I brought lunch instead. It's the least I could do after you helped me out during my time of need," he said with a chuckle, running a hand across his stubbled chin.

"Well, thank you." I glanced behind me. "Do you...do you want to come inside?"

His face wrinkled and he shrugged his shoulders. "Oh. No, I don't want to bother you."

"It's no bother," I assured him, taking a half step back. "I mean, unless you have work to do."

"Well, I do. But...I'm at a stopping point." He paused, checking briefly over his shoulder, then nodded decisively. "Actually, that sounds nice. Yes, I'd like to come in."

I stepped backward, letting him inside my house. "I'll get

us some plates..." I led the way through the sun-soaked living room and into the small galley kitchen. "So, how have you been? How was your trip?"

"Oh, it was fine."

"Just fine?"

I pulled two ceramic plates down from the cabinet near the refrigerator and reached for the bag in his hands.

"Yeah, I'm not much on Chicago. Big cities in general, really." He shrugged, resting against the cabinet. "But it is what it is. I'm just glad to be home."

"Well, we're glad you're home, too." I couldn't bear to look at him as I said it, or I'd risk going into a rant about how I meant *we're* collectively. The entire neighborhood. Not just me. Of course, I was glad too... My cheeks burned from embarrassment over a conversation that was only happening in my head.

"Well, thanks." He paused as I poured the spaghetti onto our plates, then tore open a drawer and retrieved two forks. I placed them gently on the plates, sliding them under the pasta so they wouldn't fall. "Hey, and thanks for checking on Lizzie while I was gone too."

"Oh, it was no problem," I assured him. "She was fine. I told her she could come over and sleep in the guest room if she wanted, but...I think maybe that was a weird offer. I'm not great with kids. Even worse with teenagers, unfortunately."

He lightly rapped his fingers against the countertop absentmindedly. "I'm sure you were fine."

I turned, handing his plate to him and gesturing toward the table. Before we could sit, I moved a grocery sack, two receipts, and a hair tie from the center of the table.

"Sorry about the mess." I set my plate down and brushed hair from my face. "Do you want something to drink?"

He gave a lopsided grin, sinking into his chair. "Well, I'd ask for coffee, but I heard some annoying neighbor took all you had left."

I rolled my eyes playfully. "That guy is the *worst*."

"I'll take whatever you have. Water's fine."

I poured us each a glass of water before joining him at the table. "So, how's work?"

This felt surprisingly domestic.

And awkward.

I wasn't good with this sort of thing. After my divorce, I'd been glad to think I might never have to deal with a man again. After the way things had changed so quickly with Allen, gone downhill so fast, I had no desire to set myself up for anything like that again.

That had all been nearly two years ago, and the bitter taste had still not completely disappeared from my mouth.

My relationship with Shane—whatever it was, there was no official name for it—had developed slowly. A year ago, when he and his daughter Lizzie had moved in next door, I'd done my best to avoid him entirely. He was the last person I'd expected to strike up a friendship with.

But we had.

One conversation over the backyard fence at a time.

Now, I was who he asked to check in on his daughter when he was out of town. He was who I called when I had a problem around the house that I'd have once gone to Allen for.

He borrowed my coffee.

I offered advice when he needed to replace his couch or paint the dining room.

If we passed each other outside, we always said hello.

Occasionally, we ate a meal together or shared a glass of wine.

That was it, really. The extent of our relationship. In some ways, I felt delusional for calling it a relationship, even to myself, but I didn't know what to call it.

He was a widower, I was divorced, and we'd learned to count on each other for the things our spouses were no longer around to help with.

We understood each other in a way so few people did. The grief I felt over my failed marriage recognized something in Shane. Our pain brought us together.

It was different, of course.

His was worse.

Allen had chosen to leave me. Shane's late wife had no choice.

And so, whatever this was, I needed it. I needed a friend.

As much as I loved Bethany and Lakynn, with their perfect marriages and perfect families, I could never relate to them on the level they related to each other.

They understood all of the mom stuff I never would.

They could double date.

There were milestones and rites of passage to which I'd never be privy. And, as left out as that made me feel sometimes, I had to understand it.

I cleared my throat, realizing he was still waiting for an answer, but just as I started to answer, my phone buzzed in my pocket.

"Sorry." I pulled it out, checking the screen and then

glancing next door, as if I could see Lakynn through the walls. "It's Lakynn. Give me just a sec."

"Of course." He twirled his fork in his spaghetti with an understanding nod.

"Hello?"

"Did you see it?"

"See what?"

"The car! Hurry, check your window!"

"The what?" I moved toward the window quickly.

"I saw it on my doorbell camera. A white sports car. It wasn't anyone I know. Maybe it's the new owner. Do you see anything?"

Once I'd reached the windows, I searched the street and driveway for any sign of the white sports car. All I could see were construction crews working in clusters around the house for what looked like the start of a fence installation. "I don't see anything."

She sighed. "I must've taken too long to call. Okay, well, keep your blinds open and let me know if you see anything."

It sounded ridiculous, but it would be a lie to say I wasn't just as curious as she was. Our lives were relatively normal and quiet. This new addition to our neighborhood and all the chaos and busyness they'd brought with them was the most exciting thing we'd seen in a long time.

"Maybe I'll go over and knock on the door," I offered.

"We can all go this evening. I have a photo shoot on a new product this afternoon, but after that, I'm free. We could go as soon as Bethany gets off."

"What if they leave before then? I'll just run over really quick and say hello. Then we can go again this evening. I'm not busy right now, and this could be our only chance."

She hesitated. "Are you sure you're okay to go alone?"

"Shane's here. I'll bring him with me."

"Ooh," she teased. "Well, no wonder you didn't see the car. You were *distracted*."

I checked behind me to make sure he hadn't followed me into the living room, mortified with worry that he might've heard her. "I'll see you later."

"Text me with what you find out."

"I will."

"And if it's Patrick Dempsey, I call dibs."

I grinned. "Noted."

"Okay, I've gotta go. Call me back."

When I made it back into the kitchen, Shane was obviously fighting against the urge to ask what that had been about.

"Everything okay?"

I sighed, patting the table. "Want to go on an adventure?"

He placed his fork down, staring at me as he wiped his hands and dabbed the corners of his mouth with a napkin. "I thought you'd never ask." He chuckled, standing up and pushing in his chair. "Where are we going?"

"Lakynn saw a car headed to the new neighbors' house. I thought we'd go over and introduce ourselves."

He dusted crumbs from the front of his shirt. "Okay, sure. Um, should we bring something?"

My eyes scanned the empty countertops. "I have a bottle of wine, but I always feel bad about that. What if they don't drink?"

"Fair enough. Well, I don't think it's necessary—"

"Oh. I have an idea."

"You do?"

I nodded, moving back toward the door and slipping my tennis shoes on. "Come on."

"Are you going to tell me where we're going?" he asked, following me out the door and shutting it behind him.

"If there's one person I can always count on to have something worthy of giving away at their house, it's Beth."

Realization swept over his expression. "And Leo's home."

"Mhm. She has to have some sort of cake or something."

"Funny. I can't picture Bethany having cake."

I bristled slightly at the comment. Was he saying so because she was in such great shape? She was beautiful, there was no doubt, and he had every right to say so, but—

"Being a dentist, I mean," he added briskly.

Worry replaced the anger I'd been feeling. Had my thoughts been written all over my face?

"Right," I covered quickly, as if I'd totally understood what he'd meant. "Well, her mom—have you met Siu?"

He shook his head.

"Hm. She's around quite a bit. I'm surprised you haven't been introduced. Anyway, she's a great cook. She's always bringing random stuff over. Cakes and casseroles, plus tons of authentic Korean dishes. I'm going to call her really quickly." We were nearing her porch when I pulled out my phone and dialed her number. If she was between patients, she'd be able to answer, but that was rare. I knocked on the front door just as she picked up.

"Hello?"

"Hey, random, but do you have anything we can give the new neighbor as a reason to go over there?" I checked over my shoulder, watching the construction workers buzzing around the perimeter of the house.

"Is someone there?" Her voice went an octave higher.

"Lakynn saw someone drive by in a white sports car. Shane and I are going to introduce ourselves, but I don't have anything to bring. I thought you might." I could see the dark outline of Leo approaching the door through the glass. "Actually, I see Leo now."

"What?"

He pulled the door open, running a hand through his shaggy red hair—more gray than red these days. "Everything okay?"

I put the phone on speaker. "Sorry. I knocked because I didn't think Bethany would answer, but I didn't want to come over without having called first. I need to borrow something."

He stepped back, eyeing the two of us with confusion. "Something?"

"Something to take to the new neighbor."

"Oh." He still seemed confused.

Bethany spoke loudly over the line. "Am I on speaker?"

"Yep."

"Leo, can you check in the refrigerator and see if there are any of the dishes Mom brought over that are still untouched?"

He led the way through the house. On the way, I stepped over a backpack, around three separate pairs of shoes and two controllers, and around their husky, Max.

Bethany was one of the most organized people I knew. She left the house every morning at exactly 7:05. She still ironed her clothes. Her closet was color coordinated and she had matching accessories for every outfit.

In high school, her room had always been completely clean, nothing ever out of place.

It was why it had shocked me so much when she'd married Leo, who was anything but organized. Of course, their three children had gotten her beauty and his messiness. I surveyed the living room as we moved through it, noting the open bag of potato chips on the couch and the pair of dirty socks on the floor.

I forced the thoughts away.

Leo was a nice enough guy. Despite his proclivity to clutter, he truly seemed to love Bethany. And he was a great dad. He'd taken a job working from home when the kids were younger so he could be home while she was building up her practice. And really, who was I to judge with a failed marriage of my own? I wished messes had been the worst issue for Allen and me.

"We have some of those sweet cake things," he said after a moment, shuffling things around in the fridge.

"No, those have peanuts and we don't know if anyone in their house has an allergy," Bethany said. "Keep looking."

"That's all I see in here," he said, glancing around the kitchen while scratching his stomach. "We have this gift card Jacob got for his birthday."

"We can't give the neighbors a gift card," she said firmly. "Oh, what about the brownies on the table? You didn't let the kids eat any this morning, did you?"

He turned his head slightly, checking the table just as we did. "No, but...I mean—"

"Take those," she said sharply, cutting him off.

I felt almost guilty doing so. "Are you sure?"

Leo scratched the back of his neck, then crossed the room and picked up the pan of brownies, covered in aluminum foil.

"Positive," she said, her tone cheery. "Call me and tell me what you find out, okay?"

I lifted the pan with one hand. "You've got it." I ended the call and offered Leo an apologetic smile. "Sorry about this."

"Oh, it's fine. I didn't need them anyway." His response seemed earnest, but I couldn't help thinking I'd ruined his afternoon plans. "I should get back to work, though."

"Right. I'll, uh, we'll just see you later, then."

"Yep." He saluted me with two fingers, nodding at Shane as we turned toward the door. Once we were back outside, Shane shook his head.

"Leo's a...nice guy, isn't he?" he asked, keeping his voice low. It seemed like he wanted to say more, but was refraining.

"He is," I confirmed. "Very nice and very funny."

"Funny?" He seemed surprised.

"Yep. You wouldn't know it, but he's really funny once you're around him. It's more of a dry sense of humor, you know? Anyway, he's just shy."

He nodded slowly, his lips pressed together. "He's probably the one I know the least about since I moved here."

"Yeah, well, Henry's the extrovert. Always has been. He can make friends with anyone he comes across. Lakynn, too. Less so than Henry, maybe, but she's always been the *it* girl, even when we were in high school. Bethany's not shy, but she's..." I searched for the right word. "Choosy, I guess. Once she loves you, she loves you. But it takes a while for her to warm up. And she's never afraid to let you know what she thinks of things. Leo's quieter, but always kind, and just as fun once he's comfortable with you."

"And what about you?"

"Me?" I studied him.

"You weren't the *it* girl?" he teased.

I scoffed. "Not hardly."

"Because you were shy?"

"What do you think?" I challenged.

"I'm still trying to figure you out." He scratched his chin, obviously thinking. "I mean, I was the one to talk to you first, so I'd want to say you're pretty introverted, but I've seen the way you are with your friends—"

My jaw dropped open. "What way am I?"

"You don't seem to shut up." He paused, then chuckled.

"I'll pretend not to take offense to that."

"No offense intended. I've always preferred people who can carry a conversation."

A corner of my mouth upturned involuntarily. "I don't know what I am, honestly."

"What do you mean?"

"Well, before, I would've said I was extroverted. Maybe not like Lakynn and Henry. I won't strike up conversations with strangers or anything, but I have no problem talking to people I don't know if I have to. And now, I mean, I can make phone calls and set doctor's appointments and...you know, talk in front of groups of people without a problem. But, I don't know, as I've gotten older, I find myself less and less inclined to talk to anyone. Maybe I'm getting cynical. Sometimes I think I hate people."

He scowled. "Oh, don't do that."

"Do what?"

He inhaled, pressing a finger to his lips as he appeared to contemplate his next words. "Within the last, I don't know, decade, I'd say, it's become this cool thing to say you hate people. Social media has become this cesspool of anger and reminders of how awful people are, but... I don't know. I can't *hate* people, you know? I'm not saying there aren't awful people out there, sure, but really, to hate people as a whole? I don't know. It just seems like people don't really think that statement through when they make it. I like to think the world is more good than bad." Splotches of pink covered his neck, and he shook his head. "Wow. I don't know where that came from. Thanks for coming to my TED Talk, I guess."

I chuckled. "Okay, well, fine, maybe I don't hate people. But I don't seek out chances to spend time with many of them anymore."

"Except me?" He nudged me with his elbow gently, keeping his skin on mine for an extra second. I met his eye, then looked away abruptly. He cleared his throat. "No, in truth, I get it. I feel the same way."

"You do?"

"Yeah, after losing Laura, it took me a really long time to see any good in the world, you know?" He shook his head.

"I do..." I understood more than he knew. In fact, I was still there. If it wasn't for my friends, for Shane, I might've believed there was no good left.

"Anyway," he sang, easing the tension, "this is really heavy talk for approaching someone's front door." He gestured straight ahead as we neared the porch of the grand home, and I let the conversation drop, the weight of it still lingering in the air between us.

The house was made entirely of stone, with a large bay window running the full two stories, and a columned porch along the front. The roof was black metal with sharp lines and intricate detailing, red gutters, and a single solid-stone gargoyle that sat at the very top.

When Bethany's and Lakynn's kids were young, they were all terrified of the gargoyle, until Tom and Eleanor dressed it up like Santa Claus one Christmas.

Once we'd made it to the porch, surprised no one had tried to stop us, I lifted the antique bronze door knocker and rapped it against the metal plate. I took a step back, holding the pan with both hands as I rehearsed what I was going to say.

I tried to picture who might open the door. A ridiculously wealthy socialite? An elderly couple dripping with old money? Perhaps a young family—younger than me, even—who'd invested in Bitcoin, *whatever that was*, or one of the many new companies the millennials I'd worked with at my last firm were always going on about.

Money was everywhere now, it seemed. I had a few accounting clients who made hundreds of thousands making YouTube videos. Several more who were making serious money on social media with posts about shoes, unboxing items, and living a nomadic lifestyle. It seemed, if you were pretty or charismatic enough—preferably both—you could make money doing just about anything these days.

When a few moments had passed and no one came to the door, I checked with Shane, who shrugged awkwardly. I waited a bit longer, then stepped forward again, this time pressing my finger into the bronze cat doorbell Eleanor had loved so much.

I looked up, shielding my eyes from the sun as I checked the windows on the second floor.

We waited a few more minutes before Shane said, "Maybe we missed them."

"Maybe," I said, though I didn't believe it. How could we have?

"Or maybe they're in the shower. Or sleeping."

"Maybe they're crawling across the floor to avoid answering the door."

That got a genuine laugh from him. "That's what I usually do."

"That's not what you did when we came to meet you for the first time."

His eyes danced between mine, a pregnant pause hanging in the air. "Well,"—he looked away—"to be fair, I smelled Lakynn's casserole through the door and we hadn't had a home-cooked meal in more than two years."

I rolled my eyes playfully, then looked back at the door. There was still no sign of movement, no rustling of curtains or hum of a TV. If someone was home, it was obvious they weren't going to answer the door. "I guess we'll go." I took a reluctant step backward, then another, before turning around to descend the steps.

"We can try again," he offered. Then after a moment, asked, "Why are you guys so worried about who moved in, anyway?"

"Don't you want to know your neighbors?"

He shrugged. "I do know my neighbors."

"All of them, I mean."

"Sure, I guess, but I figure we'll catch them outside at some point, right? And, if not, as long as they don't cause any problems, I don't have to know who they are."

It sounded much more reasonable than I felt at that moment, as we made our way back toward my house. As we walked, I sent Bethany a text to let her know I still had the brownies and would bring them by this evening, not wanting to interrupt Leo's work again.

When I slipped my phone back into my pocket, I said, "I guess it's just because this town is so small, you know? We basically know everyone, so when we get new people to town, especially on our street, we just want to be neighborly."

"Neighborly or nosy?" he jeered.

"Maybe a little of both," I admitted, embarrassed heat filling me. I knew he was teasing, but that didn't make it easier to admit. "I just feel safe here, you know? Surrounded by people I know. We all do. It's the appeal of small towns in general, but it's really the appeal of tight-knit neighborhoods. After the divorce, I really considered moving. I wanted to, honestly. But I couldn't bear the thought of leaving the place. It's home, you know? This place. These people."

He nodded slowly. "No, I get it. I'm only kidding. I'd like to know who shares a street with my daughter."

"Exactly," I said.

"In truth, I was really glad when I met you all."

"Yeah?"

"Mhm." He chewed his bottom lip. "It's going to sound... well, pitiful, I guess, but...after Laura died, it was just Lizzie and me for so long, you know? And, she's a teenager. Practically grown, really. But there's still so much to do. And it was

24

all on me. To raise this...this person. This actual human being who I'm going to send out into the world in just a few years. And I'd felt really alone in that for so long." His eyes filled with a contagious warmth. "So, when I met you all, and you were mothers and friends and—" I tried not to let the mothers comment sting me. "You were all so kind to us. And helpful. You still are. It's just been the best thing I could've hoped for."

My smile was weak, powerless as I tried to contain my emotion. I stared at my porch as we approached it, scared to meet his eyes. "I had no idea we'd helped you so much."

"Are you kidding?" he asked, jogging up the steps to hold the door open for me. "Between keeping an eye on Lizzie for me when I have to travel, the meals you've all brought us, answering every question I have about raising a teenage girl, and the ridiculous amount of gifts— I mean, you three really make holidays out of every occasion—"

"We do." I grinned broadly.

"I've never heard of anyone getting a Saint Patrick's Day gift before."

"The green tea and Rice Krispies Treats." I clasped my hands together in front of my chest, having nearly forgotten about them. "Really we just look for any excuse to make food."

He spun around, facing me in the narrow entryway, the humor of the moment gone. "I'm serious, Piper. You've... been the best thing that's happened to Lizzie and me in a long time."

My breath caught in my chest, unsure how to respond. We'd treated Shane like one of us because that's what he was. He was a part of our neighborhood, our family, now. It

25

was the least we could do. I wanted to tell him all that, but my voice was somewhere deep in my chest, completely uncooperative.

"All of you, I mean," he added, looking away.

I'd ruined the moment. I should've said something. Anything.

Before I could correct myself, I heard the rev of an engine. At once, we both glanced out the window, checking the unfamiliar sound just in time to see the white sports car zip down the street and out of the subdivision.

CHAPTER FOUR

LAKYNN

The invitations, much like the moving trucks that brought their sender to our neighborhood, came without warning.

It was nearly a month after the mysterious new neighbors had arrived and, aside from the white sports car coming and going occasionally, we'd seen no signs of them. Of course, that was by design, with the newly constructed concrete wall around the entire property.

Before it had gone up, we'd watched the house being locked down like a fortress, cameras on every surface, and machines with unknown uses loaded inside. Then, over the course of a week, the wall had gone up and shut us out. Now, the only proof the house was still standing came from looking through the wrought iron gate at the end of the driveway.

I wanted to complain. God knows I did, but Tom and Eleanor had once been the owners and founders of the subdivision. Though they'd never formed an official home-

27

owner's association, everything went through them. Had they passed that power on to the new owners? Or were we just on our own entirely?

I'd had Henry call down to city hall once to see if they could give us any information, but there was only one woman who worked there—Gretchen—and she'd been out on vacation.

Perks of living in a small town.

Despite our confusion and frustration, I'd finally moved on and accepted that we weren't going to meet our new neighbors—whatever the reason—when I found the black envelope in our mailbox. A red ribbon had been tied around the envelope, the address filled out with a silver marker and perfectly neat handwriting.

There were no names, only our address, and I immediately feared the worst.

We were being blackmailed.

We were being sued.

Who wrote letters anymore anyway?

I carried the stack of mail into the house, already tearing into the envelope.

"What's that?" Henry asked, entering the house through the door from the garage.

"I don't know..." I trailed off as I stared at the invitation in my hand, trying to make sense of it. The first line was a fancy script.

Join Us...

It continued in a neatly typed font.

**Please join us for an exclusive dinner party
where we will finally have the opportunity to
introduce ourselves. We're so looking forward to
being a part of the neighborhood!**

**Friday, May 6th at 6 p.m.
Hosted by the Harringtons
No gifts please**

PS Please excuse our mess!

Henry read the invitation over my shoulder, then held out his hand for me to pass it to him. He read it quickly, then turned it over in his hand and checked the back.

"Please excuse our mess..." He laughed under his breath. "If that's what they call it. The Harringtons, hm?"

"Apparently." I paused, taking the invitation back and reading it once more. "It's kind of rude, isn't it?"

"Inviting us to a party?" He opened the refrigerator.

"Inviting us to a party that's in"—I checked the date on my smartwatch—"four days. Like we don't have lives."

He pulled out the pitcher of cucumber water and poured himself a glass. "Well, maybe it was last minute. You're the one who's been dying to meet them, haven't you? Why are you so upset?"

"I'm not upset," I said, then lowered my voice, realizing I did, in fact, sound upset. "I just think it's strange that we haven't seen them once, and then they send us these invitations in the mail. Why couldn't they at least hand deliver them and say hello?"

"That's a good question," he said, noncommittally. "Maybe they're shy."

"Shy enough to build a fortress around their house," I said with a snort.

He took a sip of his water, resting against the counter. "We don't have to go, you know? We can just say we had something come up."

I twisted my mouth in thought. "I didn't say I don't want to go."

"So you do want to?"

"I'll have to see."

He fought back a smile, taking another drink.

"What?"

"Nothing," he teased, turning his back to me to place the pitcher back in the fridge.

"I don't know if we'll go. Maybe we'll come up with something to do," I insisted.

"If you say so..." He trailed off, knowing me too well to buy my lies.

"I just think it's rude."

"Mhm." He kissed my forehead, walking past me and taking a seat at the island. "We'll do whatever you want to."

I nodded, placing the invitation down. "Do you think they invited everyone on our street?"

He plucked an apple from the bowl in the center of the island, eyeing it thoughtfully. "I would hope so. It'll be pretty awkward if not. Maybe they invited the whole subdivision."

"That's hundreds of people."

"There'd be room to spare there, especially if they're planning to entertain outside." He took a bite of the apple, chewing pensively.

30

"I'll ask the girls if they got invitations, too. Then we can figure out a plan."

He pushed up from his seat, taking another bite of the red fruit in his hand. "Plan away."

He thought I was being silly, maybe, but my feelings were hurt after the way they'd ignored us. They didn't owe us anything, I knew, but this was the way things worked in small towns. It wasn't as if I expected a dinner invitation. I simply wanted to see their faces, say hello.

This... This felt wrong.

Cold.

Off.

I couldn't put my finger on what exactly it was, but I didn't like it.

I wish I'd listened to that instinct.

CHAPTER FIVE

BETHANY

By the time I made it home that night, it was already getting dark. Leo had dinner waiting for me, and the kids had scattered to their rooms with their plates. Like usual, I knew it was likely I wouldn't see them again until right before bed. Though I knew it was ridiculous, there were days when it felt like I never saw my children. They were grown now—the oldest moved out and into a college dorm, and the youngest two were teenagers with lives of their own. There were days when I was grateful to no longer feel guilty for having to work so much, but I couldn't help the worry that came with seeing them less and less. When I was a teen, my mother had been much more attentive and I still managed to get into trouble. I just had to hope my children were smarter than I'd been.

"Hey," Leo said, looking up from his phone when he saw me reenter the dining room. "How was work?"

"It was fine. How was your day?"

"Oh, it was okay." My plate was already made and

waiting for me on the counter, so I picked it up, sprinkling a bit of salt and pepper on my green beans before walking toward the table.

"Have you talked to Lakynn?" he asked, following close behind me.

"No. Should I have?"

"She was going to call you." He ran a hand over his beard. "Probably hasn't had the chance yet. Anyway, it's nothing serious. Don't look so worried." He tossed an envelope toward me from the stack of bills at one end of the table. "The neighbors that just moved in are having a dinner party."

I tried to process what he'd said as I carefully opened the black envelope. "What? When?"

"This weekend. The invitation just came in the mail."

"We're supposed to go to Mom's this weekend." I read through the invitation, running my fingers across the fancy script.

"Yeah." He shrugged, picking up a knife finally and digging into the meat on his plate. "I told her we probably won't be able to go—"

"Told who? You talked to the neighbor?" I eyed him.

His brows drew down in confusion for a minute as he chewed, then swallowed. "Oh. No. Sorry. I told Lakynn. She was here earlier, to see if we'd gotten an invitation. She didn't know you were working late tonight. Anyway, I told her we were supposed to go to your mom's house for the weekend, so we most likely wouldn't get to go. Probably for the best anyway. Their invitation seems kind of stuffy, doesn't it? Why not just come around and invite us all in person?"

I placed the invitation back in the envelope. "It's weird,

you're right. And they aren't addressed to us. Did they just send them to every address on our street?"

"No idea." He dipped his steak in sauce, popping a bite into his mouth. "Lakynn and Henry were invited, but I don't know about anyone else."

"But you don't want to go?" I asked.

His upper lip curled in disgust. "Do you?"

"I don't know what I want to do. I mean, I wanted to meet them originally, but they haven't exactly seemed open to meeting us... That concrete wall is atrocious."

He nodded in agreement, a smear of barbecue sauce on his chin. "The worst."

"I feel like I live next door to a prison."

"I agree. I never thought I'd miss Tom and Eleanor."

I scoffed. "And, like you said, we already have plans. It's such short notice."

"Yep, it is. I say we just don't go. It's not the end of the world."

"Is Lakynn going?"

"She didn't say."

I picked up my fork finally, running the tines over my food. "I mean, we do have plans."

"We do."

"But Mom would understand if we needed to reschedule. Or go there Saturday morning instead of Friday night."

He shrugged, his tone apprehensive. "It's up to you. But I don't think I have anything to wear. I doubt I fit into my old suit."

"We'll figure out something," I said. "But I'll talk to Lakynn first. If she's not going, we certainly won't."

He nodded, not saying anything else.

Despite my curiosity, I'd all but forgotten about the new neighbors over the last few weeks. I was busy enough at work that they'd become the last thing on my mind.

But with this invitation came new questions:

Who were they, after all?

Why did they want to meet us?

Why all the formality?

What would the party be like?

Would I regret going?

Would I regret not?

CHAPTER SIX

PIPER

I was working on a file for a bookkeeping client from the back patio on Friday morning when I heard noise coming from next door. I looked over, staring at Henry and Lakynn's house.

No one should've been home in the middle of the day.

Henry was at the pharmacy. Lakynn should've been at her office.

I waited, trying to see if I'd hear it again. When I didn't, I turned my attention back to the file, convinced it had been the wind.

Just as I found my focus once more, I heard the sound again.

Shhhhhh...

The sound of something scraping across concrete was unmistakable. I stood from my chair and approached the fence, peering over.

"Oh." I released a relieved sigh. "Thank God."

Henry turned his head, apparently as shocked by me as I

was by him. He was bent over at the waist, dragging a tote from their storage shed. "Hey, stranger." His expression warmed, flooding with ease. "I didn't see you there."

"I was working on the patio and heard a noise. Figured I'd better investigate."

He pulled the tote the rest of the way, shutting the door behind him. "Sorry if I bothered you." He swiped the back of his arm across his forehead. "Lakynn asked me to get some backdrops out of storage for a new campaign they're doing. She couldn't get away from work." He nudged the tote with his foot. "I just hope they're in here because I've searched everywhere else."

"Need any help?" I offered.

"Nah." His nose wrinkled. "Thanks though. I'm sorry if I interrupted you."

"Of course. It was no bother." I nodded, then turned to walk away, but he stopped me.

"Hey, are you going to the dinner party tonight?"

I spun back to face him. "I..." My upper lip curled involuntarily. The last thing I wanted to do was spend time at a party. Let alone a couples party with the new neighbors and my friends, and me being the only one there alone. But I couldn't tell them that. I'd been putting off giving them an answer. "I'm not sure. I'm swamped with work, honestly. I may just stay in to catch up, and let you guys report back on what they're like."

He nodded, shoving a hand in his pocket. "We could do that..." He trailed off, his expression unreadable.

"Everything okay?"

"Mhm." He picked up the tote, visibly struggling under

its weight. "I should get this inside and let you get back to work. We'll see you later, okay?"

"See you later." I waved a hand over my head as he turned back toward the house. As I made my way back toward the patio, I heard someone knocking on my front door. I course-corrected, moving toward the gate and peering over.

When I saw Shane, I waved at him over the fence. "I'm back here."

He searched for my voice, and his gaze landed on me finally. "Hey!"

"I'm working in the backyard." I held the gate open for him. "Everything okay?" He was empty-handed this time, so he wasn't coming for lunch. As he walked past me, I caught the sheen of sweat on his temples. He seemed pale, almost sickly.

"What? Oh-oh, yeah. Yeah. Yes. Everything's great." He rubbed a hand across the back of his neck. I kept an eye on him as I shut the gate. "Um..." When he'd reached the table, he tapped a finger on it, then turned back to me. "I'm sorry if I made things awkward. I totally understand if I did. I've been kicking myself all morning about it. It's too soon, right?" He was pacing then. And rambling. "It's *way* too soon. And I'd never want things to be weird between us because you've been so incredible with everything and I don't know what I was thinking, it was just—"

"*Shane*," I said, loudly enough to stop him in his tracks.

"Sorr—"

"What are you talking about?"

"I-uh..." The wrinkle in his forehead deepened. "Well, I was... I mean, the text. I was talking about the text. I didn't hear back from you, and I... Of course I didn't. It's totally okay. I don't know what I was thinking. It's not the sort of thing you text, right? Hell, I don't know. I'm not used to this, you know? I haven't dated in...what? Sixteen years." He dragged a hand through his hair. "Anyway, can we just forget it happened and blame it on too much time on my hands?"

"What text?" I was still trying to process everything he was saying.

"The...text...I...sent...you..." He spoke slowly, as if realization was setting in. "You didn't get it?" He looked skeptical. Relieved, maybe.

I patted my pocket, then searched the table. "I've been working outside all day. I guess I left my phone somewhere inside."

"Oh." He blanched, then gave a sheepish smile. "Well, okay then. Um..."

"What did you text me?"

He sighed. "Well, this is embarrassing. I asked if you wanted to get dinner tonight. Lizzie's staying with a friend after school and, well, I just thought...maybe we could actually have dinner outside of the house for once. But, then I didn't hear back and I started worrying you'd gotten the wrong idea or—"

"What would the *right* idea be?" I suppressed a grin.

He swallowed. Somehow, as we'd talked he'd grown even paler. As if every ounce of blood had drained from his body. "Well, what do you want it to be?"

I pursed my lips, then let out a breath. "I'd love to go to dinner with you."

"Yeah?" The color returned to his cheeks.

"Of course. We already have dinner together at least

once a week. Might as well try it out of the house and see if we're just as good there."

He laughed. "Alright. Sounds good. Does seven sound okay?"

"Yeah, whenever's good for you. I don't have any plans."

"Awesome. Okay. I'll come over and get you around seven, then. We can take my car." He patted my shoulder awkwardly, letting his hand linger on my skin, then pulled it away. "I should...let you get back to work."

"Okay." I suppressed the wide grin I could feel forming on my lips. "I'll see you tonight."

"See you tonight." He smiled with one side of his mouth, then walked away from me and toward the gate.

As he shut it, I sank into my chair, releasing a slow exhale.

Well, at least now I had an excuse not to go to the party.

CHAPTER SEVEN

LAKYNN

When I walked into the kitchen that night, dressed in a simple, royal-blue cocktail dress for the party, my son's head was buried in the refrigerator.

"What are your plans tonight?" I asked, stopping to search for a tin of mints in the junk drawer.

He pulled back to look at me, cheekful of cheese cubes. "Huh?"

"Do you have anything planned?"

He scrutinized me, his face wrinkling, and asked with a full mouth, "Why are you so dressed up?"

"Oh." I smoothed my hands over my dress. "Your dad and I have that dinner party at the neighbor's house tonight. Remember? We told you about it."

He nodded slowly, and I couldn't tell if he actually remembered or if he was just agreeing so we'd move on.

"Anyway, we shouldn't be out late. Nine-ish, probably. Will you be home?"

"Probably not." He pulled a bag of baby carrots from the

refrigerator and shut the door. "I think I might go to Max's for a while and play." He gestured toward the hard-shell guitar case that lay on the kitchen table.

"That'll be nice."

"What will?" Henry asked from behind me, his voice echoing down the hall.

"Aaron might go to Max's tonight," I informed him, dropping the tin of mints into the clutch in my hand and retrieving my favorite lipstick, a deep-mauve color. I applied it to my lips again, rubbing them together before dropping the lipstick in with the mints and snapping the clutch closed.

Henry walked around the corner, giving me an appreciative once-over. "Damn, girl."

I chuckled. "Not so bad yourself." I wasn't lying. My husband—with his golden-brown skin and kind eyes highlighted behind thick-framed glasses—appeared incredibly trim in his navy suit. He slipped a hand around my waist, pulling me into him and kissing my lips. For just a moment, we forgot where we were.

He could still do that to me. Still make everything else disappear, so the only people in the universe who existed were us.

"Ew, god, you guys—" Aaron groaned, turning to walk out of the kitchen.

Henry pulled back from me slowly. "Hey," he called over his shoulder.

Aaron turned around promptly. "Yeah?"

"What time are you going to Max's?"

"I have no idea. In a little while. Why?"

"Text us if you're planning on leaving his house and tell

us where you'll be and who you'll be with. What's your sister doing tonight?"

"I'm dropping her off at Andrea's on the way."

"Tell her to do the same then." Henry eyed Aaron suspiciously. "I mean it. If either of your plans change, we need to know *before* they do."

"Okay, okay. I already told you, we aren't planning on leaving," he said simply, shrugging one shoulder.

"Well, that's fine. But you heard me, if plans change, we need to know where you are."

He saluted his father playfully, then turned back around. "Aye, aye, sir."

Henry laughed and patted Aaron's shoulder. "Get out of here. Go have fun."

"You guys too."

I pulled my phone out, checking the group text I'd sent Bethany and Piper earlier, and gasped.

"What's wrong?"

"Well, apparently Piper isn't coming." I glanced up at him, expecting him to look just as bothered by this, but instead, he winced.

"I knew I was forgetting something. Sorry, I meant to tell you."

"You mean you knew?"

"Yeah. She mentioned it earlier when I saw her. Something about work—"

"No," I argued. "It's not work. It's Shane. They're going on a date."

"They are?" Now he seemed shocked.

"Apparently. Come on, we have to go over there."

"Go over there? Where? To Piper's?"

"We all have to go together. That was the plan."

"Whose plan?"

I furrowed my brow. "It was *the* plan. The only plan. The more people, the less awkward."

"I get that, but come on, it's not like we can't make it through an evening without Piper. Honestly, it might be easier anyway."

I stopped in my tracks, staring at him dubiously. "Why would you say that?"

He cleared his throat, urging me forward. "Nothing. Never mind."

"No," I said firmly. "Why?"

"It's just..."

"Just what?"

He turned to face me finally, letting out a sigh. "Look, I know Piper's your friend—"

"She's yours, too."

"Yeah, she is. You're right. I really like Piper. Always have. It's just that...Allen was my friend. Piper was—*is* —yours."

"What are you saying?"

"It's just kind of awkward, you know? Like, all the stuff Allen's told me since the divorce—"

"Stuff like what, Henry?"

"Nothing, really. Just stupid stuff. My point is that... Well, it's awkward with Piper because she's single, when she's always come with Allen before."

"She got a divorce, Henry. Two years ago. For goodness' sake, it's not the end of the world. If you ask me, Allen never appreciated her anyway and—"

"I'm not defending him. The way he left things sucked.

All I'm trying to say is that, well, if she's dating Shane... that's...that's a good thing, right? We should encourage it."

"I don't know about that..."

He scoffed. "What? Mrs. Matchmaker? How many times have I watched you set up people from work? Or old friends? Hell, you set up my mom with that guy from your office."

"Marco was a client and we were done with his campaign. I didn't work with him. And she liked Marco!"

He held up his hands in defeat, lowering his voice. "Look, I'm not saying you aren't great at what you do. I'm saying the opposite. You *love* love, so why wouldn't you want your friend to be happy?"

I huffed, folding my arms across my chest. "I do want her to be happy."

"You just...don't think Shane will make her happy?"

"Okay, it's not lost on me that Shane has had a crush on her for a while, and she's had a crush on him too, but...I know Piper. *We* know Piper. She's fragile right now. The divorce took so much from her. And she's just finally getting back to a good place. Whatever they've had seems healthy. And I do like Shane. I just want her to be careful." I paused. "And I want her to be careful any night *besides* tonight, because tonight, she's coming with us."

He sucked in a breath through his teeth, his chest heaving. "Whatever you say." He was skeptical, but that didn't stop him from following close behind me as I made my way toward the door.

"Don't forget the wine," I called behind me, gesturing toward the bag near the door, strategically placed so we wouldn't forget it. Seconds later, we were out the door and onto the street. Bethany was fussing with Leo's shirt collar when they saw us and waved from their front walk. They turned, headed in our direction, and we met them midway.

"Guess it's just us tonight, huh?" Leo said, hands out to his sides as if he'd just done a magic trick with a big reveal.

"No," I snipped.

"Told you." Bethany cast a knowing glance over her shoulder toward her husband. The off-the-shoulder red dress she was wearing was the same one she'd worn to my anniversary party last year, and I caught the glimmer of highlight on her cheekbones. She was effortlessly beautiful in normal clothing, but she'd always had an elegance to her that was meant to be dressed up.

Next to her, in khakis and a wrinkled dress shirt, Leo looked entirely too plain. I shuddered to wonder if people thought the same when comparing us. Was I just Bethany's plain best friend? Was I Henry's plain wife?

"We have to go talk to her," I said, refusing to let my anxiety get the better of me, as Bethany nodded along, already on board.

As if on cue, Piper's door opened and the sound of Shane's voice could be heard from where we stood.

"No, honestly, I do tend to stick with what I know, but I'm fine with trying whatever..." He trailed off when he saw us, appraising us with shock. "Evenin', ladies. Going somewhere?"

I stalked across the sidewalk toward them, my heels clicking loudly. "We're going to dinner with the new neighbors. Just like the two of you."

"We're—" He cut himself off, brows drawn down, then

looked at Piper as if he hadn't gotten some sort of memo. "We are?"

"We're not," she said, staring at me with playful disdain. "I told you, I'm going to dinner with Shane tonight. You'll have to tell me all about the fancy party tomorrow."

"But you have to come," Bethany begged. "Come on. You can't cancel on us last minute. Why can't you just have dinner together there?"

"Hang on," Shane said, obviously trying to catch up. He pointed at Piper. "Were you supposed to go to dinner with them?"

"Yes, she was," Bethany said. "You both were. You can't just leave us hanging."

Piper shook her head. "It's not a big deal. It's—"

"Wait. *Both* of us? I'm missing something. Was there a text chain I wasn't a part of? What are you talking about?" Shane asked, his gaze bouncing between the five of us.

"You didn't get an invitation?" Leo asked.

"An invitation? No, I don't think so..."

A rock sank in my stomach, burning me from the inside with embarrassment. "It probably just got lost in the mail," Henry offered halfheartedly. Once I'd found out Piper and Bethany were invited, it had never occurred to me that everyone on the street hadn't been.

"Maybe they only invited their next-door neighbors," Leo said, pointing to our houses.

"But that can't be it," I pointed out. "Piper was invited, and she's not next door."

"Yeah, but she's closer than Shane. Maybe they invited all of us and Mrs. Morgan. We'd be the closest neighbors," Leo said.

"Maybe," Shane said, his tone clipped. "Hey, why don't you go ahead and go to this tonight, and we can have dinner tomorrow night? Honestly, it's not a big deal. I don't want you to have to miss this. I know you've been excited to meet them."

"No!" Piper said. "Besides, I'm not even dressed for a party." She gestured toward the long tunic and leggings she was wearing. "I want to go with you."

At the same time, we all spouted our thoughts, trying to ease the awkwardness of the moment.

"Well, maybe you should just come."

"I'm sure it got lost."

"They'd be fine with you coming."

"And you look gorgeous, Piper," I added, and it wasn't a lie.

"Totally," Bethany added.

Shane shook his head, hand in the air to wave off our concerns. "Honestly, guys, it's not a big deal." He looked back at Piper. "We can do this any time. Maybe tomorrow night instead."

"Why don't you just come with her?" I said again, drawing his attention back to me.

He grimaced. "I'm a little old to be crashing parties, don't you think?"

"You could be her plus-one." I nodded firmly, glancing back at the house. "The invitations weren't even really addressed to anyone, and they didn't say we couldn't bring guests. Besides, like Henry said, your invitation probably just got lost. Come on. Come with us." My eyes darted between them, trying to decide who I needed to convince. "Come on. Please. You guys can go to dinner any time. How many chances are you going to have to go into this house and meet our new *mysterious* neighbors?" I wiggled my fingers in the air, as if I were an apparition.

Piper swatted my hands away with a look of playful disapproval, but I could see her wavering. She checked with Shane, her head tilted to the side slightly. "She's right. You could be my plus-one. The invitation wasn't an RSVP. For all we know, your invitation *did* get lost. And, even if it didn't, it's not like Mrs. Morgan is coming."

"Hey, don't judge," Leo joked from behind us. "I have it on good authority that Mrs. Morgan knew how to party in her day."

Shane sighed, rubbing a hand over his mouth. "I don't know."

"Come on," Bethany chimed in. "It'll be fine. Besides, you're one of us now, aren't you? One of the family." She beamed at him, and I saw the ease with which she pulled him in.

I felt the snares of jealousy intertwining in my guts.

Why was it so easy for her to win people over? I'd been able to do that once, but now, it felt like a lost art, squandered away after years of neglect.

Shane sighed, rubbing his chest. "Okay, fine. But if they're a chair short, I'm blaming one of you."

"Blame me," I offered, hand in the air. "All right, now, can we go?"

"Are you sure I look okay?" Piper asked. "Should I change first?"

"You look perfect, and we're already late," I said, nudging her forward. "Come on."

Glancing at the watch on my wrist, I led the way down the darkening street and toward the large iron gate.

We were several minutes late now, in fact, but I tried not to think of it. Or of the impression it would give.

It wasn't as if our new neighbors were the champions of a great first impression, after all.

CHAPTER EIGHT

BETHANY

The door seemed larger somehow, though I knew it was impossible. It was the same door it had always been. Only now, it was protected by a gate that had shut behind us.

A gate that had locked us inside.

Lakynn stood on the top step, obsessively smoothing her dress and fussing with her hair. Next to her, Henry was as cool as ever, his eyes taking in the architecture of the house the same way I'd been.

It had always been an impressive house, but now, it seemed different.

Once, it had been full of life. Full of the eccentricities of its previous owners.

Now, it seemed darker.

Sinister.

The kind of house you'd expect Stephen King to live in.

I was being ridiculous, I knew. Maybe it was just the unknown of what we were walking into. Of who would be waiting for us behind the door.

Leo reached out, taking my hand and sliding his fingers between mine, an enormous phony grin on his lips.

"You look beautiful, by the way."

Before I could respond, the door swung open abruptly, light from inside the home illuminating us on the dark doorstep. I blinked rapidly, attempting to decipher what I was seeing.

The couple in the doorway was beautiful; it was the first thing I noticed. So unyieldingly perfect, I thought for a moment they were statues.

Both dressed in solid black, the man wore a simple suit and tie. Simple, but expensive, I fielded a guess. The material wasn't cheap. There was nothing about this couple that appeared cheap, in fact. Not their matching, pearly white, million-dollar smiles, or their perfectly effortless hair.

A small smile formed on the woman's delicate features, causing the skin around her crystal-blue eyes to wrinkle ever so slightly. She brushed a bit of her long, dark hair over her shoulder before resting a perfectly manicured hand against the man's arm.

"Howdy, neighbors," the man said with a close-lipped smile.

The comment was so completely out of left field, it took a moment for me to grasp what he'd said. When I had, I released a breathless chuckle. Henry and Piper did the same.

"Sorry, just a little Southern joke," he said, and I detected a Northern accent. The tension eased as the man stepped out onto the porch with us, an arm outstretched to nudge us out of the way. We stepped back awkwardly, making way for him.

Wasn't he going to invite us inside?

I shot a glance toward the woman, still lingering in the doorway.

The man sucked in a deep breath, his gaze dancing over the courtyard, obviously admiring the oasis they'd built for themselves here. When he spoke, I was so lost in thought, it startled me. "What do you think of it?"

"What?" Henry asked softly, as if we'd all misheard.

The man held his hands up, gesturing toward the yard, then the house. "This place really is something, isn't it?"

"Uh, yeah, it's...it's very nice." Henry scratched the back of his neck as we all murmured in agreement.

He glanced over his shoulder at us, speaking low as if he were sharing a juicy secret. "A man's house is his castle, you know?"

"So I've heard," Henry said, tapping his foot. He did that when he was agitated; he probably hadn't even realized he was doing it.

When the man turned back to us after another pause, his jaw dropped and he swiped a hand over his eyes. "God, where are my manners? I'm so sorry." He walked toward us briskly. "I haven't even introduced myself. I'm Penn Harrington, your new neighbor. This is my wife, Etta."

He held out a hand to Henry first, who took it without hesitation.

"Henry Holmes, this is my wife—"

Penn pulled his hand back, offering it to Lakynn next.

"Lakynn," Henry finished.

"Pleasure to meet you both. And which house is yours?"

"The one right next door." Lakynn didn't bother to elaborate further.

"Blue shutters," Henry added, pointing toward their house.

Penn turned his attention to me next, holding out a hand. "I'm...Bethany. And this is my husband, Leo." When he gripped my hand, his skin was warm and dry, unlike my own cool and sweaty palm.

Normally, I would've claimed I was the most put together of our group, but something about this man had set me on edge.

He released my hand, moving down the line to shake Leo's hand, before Piper and Shane introduced themselves.

Once we'd all said hello, he gestured toward the door, one hand shoved into his pocket.

"Well then, as nice of a night as it is, I suppose we should go inside before our dinner gets cold. We do want to apologize for the slightly odd way we've handled this situation, which we'll explain further once we're inside, but we're just delighted you all could make it on such short notice." He gave another tight-lipped smile, puffing a breath of air from his nose. We turned to face the door, Henry and Lakynn leading the way inside.

Leo and I were in the back, followed closely by Penn, and I couldn't help but think of those horror movie scenes where a group goes through a dark corridor and, when they come out on the other side, the person in the back is missing.

"We love what you've done with the place," Henry called back to Penn.

"Oh, thank you. Just a bit of paint and some new fixtures really. There's plenty more we'll want to do, but this place really shines on her own."

The sensual way he spoke about his house was giving me

the creeps. I slid my hand into Leo's, anchoring myself to my husband out of sheer desperation. I was being dramatic, I knew. This was a dinner party, nothing more.

A dinner party like one I'd attended many times before.

I was going to meet my new neighbors, chat with old friends, and I'd be home by ten.

At least, that's what I thought.

CHAPTER NINE

PIPER

I'd only been inside the house a dozen or so times when Eleanor and Tom owned it, but while walking down the long, narrow hallway that led into the rest of the house, I was immediately struck by how wrong everything new felt in the old space.

The Burnetts were an odd couple with strange tastes, but there was something about them that just made everything fun. Every piece of furniture in their home had been brightly colored and whimsical. Even the normal things—doorbells shaped like cats and bathroom sinks that looked like upside-down umbrellas. Odd paintings of strange faces and animals dressed like humans. A living room set of chairs that looked like hands. Chandeliers made entirely of glass shaped like those old red monkeys from the Barrel of Monkeys games. Photos of their world travels adorning all the walls, expensive collections of books in every room. There was a chair that was made entirely of old, recycled shoes, and a coffee table book that was just the fronts of old cereal and cracker boxes. They'd had music going all hours of the day and night—everything from classical music to old-school hip-hop, and they'd dance around their house and yard in their matching velour jumpsuits without a care in the world.

When the Burnetts still lived here, the house was full of life.

Now, it was closer to being a tomb.

The color had been stripped from the walls, painted bright white throughout. The only artwork that now hung on the walls was abstract paintings of black smears, streaks, and lines. Like giant Rorschach tests in every room. The furniture was new, leather, and stiff.

As we made our way through the practically silent house, I felt a pang of sadness for our old neighbors. I hadn't realized I missed them until that moment.

Wherever they were, I was sure they were having the time of their lives, so I'd try not to feel bitterness over it, but I couldn't help feeling sad for us.

If the Burnetts were still here, Tom would've greeted us at the door with beers, a quick handshake with one of his electric shock buzzers tucked in his palm, and familiar, welcoming pats on the shoulders. He would've immediately pulled the men aside to show them the latest sculpture they'd had flown in from Peru or the backstage tickets they'd gotten to a concert of a band we'd never heard of. Eleanor would've dragged us into the kitchen to try a new drink she'd concocted, and we would've all pretended it didn't taste like fingernail polish and strawberries.

Though visits with the Burnetts were never a highlight of my days, I couldn't deny how badly I missed them now.

As we entered the kitchen, Etta turned to face us, her long, black hair swaying as she did.

"Come on in, make yourselves comfortable," she said, gesturing around the island. "Can I take anything from you? Purses? Or..." She eyed the black bag currently hanging from Henry's arm.

Obviously just remembering he was still holding it, Lakynn's hand shot out, taking the bag from her husband and passing it to our host. "It's one of our local favorites. I wasn't sure what you'd be serving tonight, but it pairs well with just about everything. I'm sorry I didn't get a chance to ask if alcohol was okay. I always feel weird gifting it, but I wasn't sure about the best way to contact you..." She trailed off, eyeing our guests expectantly.

"It's perfect. That was very thoughtful of you," Penn said, moving to stand next to his wife.

"We'll open this up right now," Etta said, pulling the bottles from the bag to inspect them. "Thank you, Lakynn."

"Oh, it was nothing. It's from all of us." She waved her hands in our direction. "We didn't want to show up empty-handed."

"Well, then, thank you all," Etta added, making her way around the island to where eight wineglasses had been placed. She folded the bag gently, laying it on the counter.

"Here, I'll get that," Penn said, rushing toward her as she pulled the drawer open and began searching for a corkscrew.

Etta slid the bottles toward him and swiped her hands together, her gaze falling back to us as an awkward tension filled the room.

"So, what brought the two of you to Poe?" Henry asked,

breaking the silence as he shoved his hands in his pockets with a sigh.

Etta glanced at Penn, who'd just finished using the electric corkscrew to open the wine. He cleared his throat as he began to pour our drinks.

"Well, I'm actually from Poe, originally."

We released gasps in unison. "You are?" Lakynn asked. I knew we were all thinking the same thing. Poe was a small community. We knew nearly everyone who lived here, but I'd never met Penn before, and his name wasn't familiar.

Was he lying?

And, if so, why?

"We moved away when I was seventeen or eighteen, but I always wanted to come back." He grinned at his wife before pouring wine into the final glass. "And now we have." He lifted two glasses, moving around the island and handing them to Lakynn and Piper.

"Do we know you, then?" Henry asked as Penn passed the next glass to Etta, then another to me. "Did you go to school with us?"

"Oh, no. I doubt it," Penn said. "I was homeschooled. My parents traveled for work, so we were all over the place most of the time. Never stayed anywhere too long. But this place...I don't know how to explain it. It just always felt like home." As he spoke, he distributed the rest of the glasses among the men before slipping an arm around his wife. "And, when we made it back, I wanted to celebrate by inviting you all over for dinner and drinks to say hello and officially introduce ourselves." He tilted his head toward Etta. "My wife thought it might come across as odd, so I hope that's not the case. We've had movers and construction workers and security personnel"—he moved his head lazily from side to side as he spoke—"in and out, but we haven't been able to see the house until just two days ago. And with all the, er, changes we're doing to the lot, we thought it would be best to meet with you all as quickly as possible. Which was the reason for the invitations."

Etta chuckled, rolling her eyes. "Which I told him were the creepiest things ever."

"She did," he admitted.

"Well, since you brought it up, I hope it's okay to ask..." Leo said, his voice soft, ears bright red. He cracked his knuckles over and over—*crack, crack, crack*—as a knot formed in my stomach. "What's up with the wall and all the security and stuff?" He twirled his finger in the air as he asked it, glancing around as if searching for hidden cameras.

For a moment, everyone was silent. I tried to gauge Penn's reaction. Was that too intrusive? Would he think Leo was rude? In my experience with Leo, I understood he wasn't trying to be rude, but rather, he was genuinely curious and he seemed to lack any sense of boundaries.

"You don't have to answer that," Bethany chided, her jaw tight.

"No, it's okay, we don't mind," Etta said, waving off the concern. "I'm sure it's been quite a shock for you all and we're sorry about that—"

"Yes," Penn said, patting her side. "Right. We are sorry. Usually, when we move, we've had a chance to introduce ourselves to the neighbors and prepare them for what's to come. Unfortunately, because of the way things worked out with our scheduling, that just wasn't possible this time. We appreciate your patience with us and I'm pleased to say all construction is now complete, so any further renovations should be to the interior, which will only affect us." He paused, then seemed to catch his train of thought. "Oh, but as for what the security is there for, well, obviously, it's for our protection. As I mentioned, my family and I have moved around quite a bit because of the line of work we're in. I can't go into details on that, unfortunately. But...we're not criminals." He chuckled to himself, making me think they definitely *were* criminals. "And, um, we won't be putting you into any danger. Anyway, it's tacky to talk about money, but we've had robberies before. People breaking in to steal from us. There was an..." His gaze flicked to Etta, then to his drink. "An attack a few years ago—"

"Oh my god." I gasped at the same time as Lakynn.

"I'm so sorry."

"We're okay," he said firmly. When I glanced at Etta, there was a coldness to her stance that assured me what he was saying was true. She looked as if she was on the brink of collapse. "We're okay," he repeated. "We're here. And...well, I will make sure that doesn't happen again, even if I'm going a little overboard."

The ice in Etta's gaze melted and she looked down, blinking out of her trance, then reaching for her husband's arm. She squeezed it once, something unspoken passing between them.

"Anyway, enough about the past. Tonight is about good food, great drinks, and new friends," she said, raising her glass and waiting for us to do the same.

We joined her in the toast. As I sipped my wine, the familiar warmth filling my chest, I tried to fight down the guilt I felt over judging them so harshly before.

What was working from home and living alone turning me into?

Why was I so nervous?

"This wine is delicious, Lakynn," Etta told her, taking another sip as if to prove it. "You'll have to tell me where to get more."

"I'll write it down for you," she promised. "They have a website, but you really should go down to visit the winery. They're amazing."

"Oh, I'd like that. Maybe we could all go together." She smiled, checking with each of us.

"I'm in," I said.

"I'd love that," Lakynn agreed.

"Count me in," Bethany said, though I couldn't help noticing she didn't sound entirely convinced.

"Perfect." She drained the last of her wine from her glass. "All right, now who's hungry?"

I opened my mouth to answer, but was cut off instantly. It took a half second for my brain to register what I was hearing, but I saw the fear in everyone's eyes, convincing me I was right.

As we stood there, sipping wine and toasting our upcoming meal, a bloodcurdling scream tore through the house.

CHAPTER TEN

LAKYNN

"What was that?" I asked, staring down the long hallway toward the bedrooms. The scream had stopped, but it was still echoing in my ears. The voice was unfamiliar and animallike. The sound sent chills down my spine.

"Oh." Etta covered her dark-red lips with one hand, shaking her head. "I thought you turned that thing off?" She elbowed her husband.

He cleared his throat, adjusting the button of his suit jacket. "I thought so, too. Excuse me for just a moment." His tone was tense, body rigid, as he jogged down the dimly lit hall and away from us.

"It's something the old owners left behind. Some sort of clock that makes weird noises every hour. Screams, shrieks, giggles." She rolled her eyes, checking the watch on her slender wrist. "It's bolted to the wall and we have tried everything to get it removed, but it's looking like we'll have to call in a professional."

I didn't know the clock she was talking about, but it didn't surprise me a bit. That sounded like exactly the sort of thing Tom would've found hilarious.

"Tom always had a thing for clocks," Leo said, looking as relieved as I'm sure we all felt. I nodded. He was right. In fact, as we made our way into the dining room, I realized how much larger it felt without Tom's wall of ornate grandfather clocks.

"I can't imagine why he left this thing behind, then," she said dryly.

"They left in kind of a hurry," Piper said, though none of us acknowledged it.

"Did they?" Etta asked. "How strange."

In the dining room, I admired the intricately set double-pedestal table. The plates were rimmed with gold, and surrounded by silverware whose uses I couldn't field guesses for. In front of each plate was another wineglass and a smaller water glass. In the center, a stainless steel wine cooler shaped like an elaborate serving bowl held five additional bottles of wine.

I ran a hand over my arms, trying to quiet the goose bumps that still lined my skin from the scream just as Penn reappeared.

"Did you get it taken care of?"

Penn swiped sweat from his otherwise perfect forehead. "The switch was off, but apparently that's not enough to keep that thing quiet." He waved his hand in the air nonchalantly. "I just flipped the breaker for that entire room. We'll deal with it later, after our guests have gone home."

Etta's smile was tense, but eventually, she nodded, then

turned to us with a gracious smile. "Of course. Feel free to sit wherever you'd like."

"This is lovely," Piper chimed in, her voice breathless.

"Oh." Etta waved her off. "Thank you, but I can't take any credit. Mrs. Doyle did it all."

"Who's Mrs—" Leo began to ask, but was promptly interrupted by a woman dressed all in white entering the room, as if on cue. She was short and plump, with deep-green eyes and her graying hair cut above her ears.

"Right on time," Etta said, grinning at her. They were polar opposites in every way, and I couldn't help finding it amusing to see them stand next to each other.

"Good evening, all," Mrs. Doyle said. "I'll be bringing out the food in just a moment, but first I wanted to be sure there aren't any food allergies I should be aware of? I've made honey roast duck with a balsamic mushroom spinach salad, but I've got plenty of other options that I can whip up in no time, should I need to." She glanced around, checking with each of us.

"That sounds delicious."

"Sounds good to me."

"Oh, yum. I've never tried duck."

"No allergies here."

Once she was satisfied, she nodded, clasping her hands in front of her. "Excellent, well, please have a seat, and I'll serve dinner momentarily."

"Thank you, Mrs. Doyle," Penn said, moving to the head of the table. He held out the seat next to his and Etta made her way toward it.

"Our housekee..." Etta looked at Penn with an odd expression on her face as she sank into the chair. "Well, I'm really not sure what to call her anymore. We hired her as a housekeeper initially, with a few house manager duties like bills and such, but she quickly became our chef as well. She makes the most delicious meals, and Penn and I are absolutely hopeless in the kitchen."

"Which Mrs. Doyle realized when she saw how much we were spending on dining out," Penn added with a laugh.

Once Etta was seated, Penn waited for the rest of us to claim our spots, standing patiently behind his own chair. For a moment, we each exchanged glances. Without waiting for anyone to make the first move, Henry hastened toward Etta, squeezing between Shane and Piper and reaching for his chair.

"Excuse me," I said, as I followed suit, pulling out the chair next to Henry and taking a seat.

To an onlooker, I suppose it might've looked suspicious—they might expect me to feel jealous of the way my husband rushed forward to claim his seat, making no small show of his determination to sit next to our host—but I felt no jealousy as I sat down. For one thing, I highly doubted I had anything to worry about with Henry. We'd been together since high school, and he'd never given me any reason to doubt his loyalty. For another, I knew my husband, which meant I knew that above all else, he wanted to be liked by everyone we met. I suspected his desire to sit near the head of the table had little to do with Etta, despite her beauty, and everything to do with getting to know Penn and Etta as a couple better. Though he'd never admit his goal, I knew it. I understood my husband without him having to say a word. There was nothing callous or vindictive about the way he strived to make sure the Harringtons favored him.

Add that to the fact that Etta and Penn were a perfectly matched duo, and I was happy to sit wherever my husband placed us. Relief swam through me when Bethany took a seat at the opposite end of the table from Penn, directly next to me. At least that meant I'd have someone to talk to if the dinner became awkward.

Leo sat down next to Bethany and across from me, smiling at us both awkwardly. With just two available seats left, Piper quickly sat down next to Leo, leaving Shane to take the seat between her and Penn.

"Now then, how's everyone doing on wine?" Penn asked, swirling his empty glass. "Ready for a refill?"

He refilled the empty glasses with one of the bottles from the table as Mrs. Doyle zipped back into the room with plates of food.

"These are very hot," she warned, placing the first two down and retreating in a hurry. Within minutes, she'd delivered each of our plates and took a step back. "Is there anything else I can get for you?"

A few of us shook our heads, to which she gave a resigned nod. "Very well. Enjoy." She addressed Etta next. "I'll go clean up, but let me know if anyone should need anything."

"Thank you, Mrs. Doyle," Etta said with a warm smile.

I'd never eaten duck before, but I couldn't deny the way the meat had my mouth watering. It was only then I realized my busy schedule that day had kept me from eating anything. I'd have to go easy on the wine.

"These are plated so beautifully," Bethany said, moving her fork across her food as she surveyed the meal.

"Mrs. Doyle's the best," Penn agreed. "There's a reason

I've gone up a pant size since she started doing the cooking around here."

Judging by the sight of his trim figure, I doubted very much that he'd ever gone up a pant size, but I let him have the joke.

"So, tell us more about yourselves," Etta said, changing the subject. "What do you all do for a living? Have you lived in Poe all your lives? How did you meet?"

"We go way back," Henry answered for us. "We've known each other since elementary school."

"Except me," Shane interjected. "I just moved here last year."

"Right," Henry agreed. "So, yeah, everyone except Shane. The rest of us are born and bred Poevillians." He laughed at his own joke. "We got closer as we got older. Lakynn and I were high school sweethearts. Leo and Bethany, too. Well, they got together right before graduation, but we let 'em have it." He took a bite of his food, chewing thoughtfully. "And we always dreamed of living in this neighborhood, but the houses here just never come on the market. So, when we saw these two for sale across from each other, we had to have them."

"Piper's house came available the next year, and we were all together again," I added.

"Mhm," Henry went on, chewing the last of his food before speaking. "And I own the pharmacy on the square. And my wife's the director of marketing for a local skincare brand. Have you heard of Merit?"

Heat rushed to my cheeks instantly. Not because I was ashamed of my job, but because I hated when Henry doted on me. I knew he was doing it to be nice, so I rarely said anything, but if it were up to me, he'd just say I'm in marketing and move on. Of course, that wasn't my husband's style.

"I can't say that I have," Etta said, after thinking for a moment.

"You'll have to check them out. It was a small little mom-and-pop store for the longest time run by two local sisters. Then they hired Lake and now they've gone national!" He glanced over at me, nodding enthusiastically.

"That's wonderful!" Etta exclaimed, leaning forward and tilting her glass toward me.

"Thanks," I said softly.

"And what about the rest of you?" Penn prompted, sending relief coursing through me.

"Bethany owns a dental practice," Leo said proudly. "And I'm in insurance."

"Writer," Shane chimed in, raising two fingers in the air.

"A writer? How interesting. Have you written anything I would've read?" Etta asked.

"Probably not," Shane said quickly, waving her off. "It's mostly freelance stuff."

"And what about your wife?" Penn asked, gesturing toward Piper, who blanched. She looked at Shane, then Penn, her eyes wide.

"Oh, I'm not—"

"She's not my—"

They spoke over each other, too loudly, then both froze, laughing too loudly. God, I was glad I'd gotten the awkward stuff out of the way in high school. Finally, Shane shook his head, meeting Penn's eye once more.

"Sorry, Piper's not my wife. We're just friends."

"Ah, I see. My bad," Penn said quickly. "I just assumed."

"I invited him as my plus-one," Piper added. "I hope that's okay. The invitation didn't say whether we should bring someone, but since everyone else was coming as a couple, and Shane and I are single, it seemed like it would be okay..." She was breathless, still pale, and I noticed her tucking her shaking hand under the table. Was she still nervous because she was worried about inviting Shane without permission? Or just shaken over the assumption that she was his wife?

"Of course. Yes, the more the merrier. I'm just sorry we didn't get to invite you ourselves, Shane. Do you live in Poe, then?"

He'd just taken a bite when they asked, so he chewed quickly, a small smile on his face. He glanced at Piper, willing her to answer for him, which she did.

"He lives next door to me, actually. It was another reason I invited him. He's one of the neighbors, too."

"Oh, that's great!" Etta said, her tone almost patronizing. "Well, I hope you aren't too offended that we didn't invite you. We thought it would be best to invite the four houses closest to us, since we didn't know what kind of turnout we'd get and we wanted to keep it intimate."

"Well, you invited Mrs. Morgan, then," Bethany said with a sly grin to Leo, who'd guessed that exact scenario earlier in the night. "She lives next to us, and she's in her nineties."

"Oh!" Etta covered her mouth, her eyes wide. "Well, then I'll try not to be too offended that she didn't come tonight," she teased.

"I'm sure she's already in bed," Bethany said. "But don't be fooled. She's sprightly for her age."

"Still mows her own lawn and wouldn't even let me come over to help change her light bulbs," Leo agreed. "She's a firecracker."

"Either way, we're glad you could join us, Shane," Penn said simply, lifting his drink to his lips. "Glad you all could join us."

"So, tell us more about yourselves. Do you have kids? Pets?" Bethany asked, and I was relieved that someone else was as curious as I felt about our elusive hosts.

"Oh, no," Etta said, waving one hand in the air while the other covered her stomach as if protecting it from such a wild idea. "It's just the two of us. We're much too busy to keep even plants alive, let alone anything else."

"So, you travel a lot, then?" Bethany asked, her tone pointed. She was determined now, and if there was one thing I knew about my best friend, it was how hard it was to stop her once she had her mind set on anything.

"Well, a fair bit, yes," she said, giving a pointed stare in her husband's direction. "But..." She drew out the word. "We're hoping that will change with our new home here. Penn's promised me he's going to take some time off so we can enjoy ourselves."

"Ahh, that I have." He reached for her hand, taking it in his and kissing her knuckles. "Aren't we enjoying ourselves tonight, darling?" he asked coyly, placing her hand back down and taking another sip of his wine.

I watched them intently, mesmerized by their every move. Etta pressed her lips together, and I sensed there were underlying issues attempting to surface, some sort of unspoken conversation happening before our very eyes. There didn't seem to be a lot of love between Penn and Etta, I was realizing. Though they'd touched each other more often this evening than Henry and I had, or Bethany and Leo for that matter, I still sensed something was off with them.

Then again, maybe I was still just a bit paranoid about the scream.

CHAPTER ELEVEN

BETHANY

I didn't buy a minute of their phony, perfect little facade.

As the evening passed, we sank further into conversation, everyone finding a sort of ease with Etta and Penn that I couldn't understand.

Henry, of course, because that was in his DNA.

And Leo was a puppy dog who loved everyone.

But I was disappointed in Lakynn and Piper, who didn't seem to be feeling any of the unease that I was filled with. I'd spent most of dinner trying to catch their eyes, waiting for a signal that they didn't trust these people either, but no such signal came.

Didn't they notice the way Penn kept checking the time anxiously? Or the way Etta's lips would tighten when they exchanged glances now and again.

Something was up.

They were lying about something.

And why couldn't they tell us about their jobs? What the

hell was going on? I wanted to kick my husband under the table to get his attention, but I knew I had to play it smart.

My only goal at that point was to figure out who the hell these people were, what they were doing in our neighborhood, and what they wanted from us.

Once we'd finished our meals, Mrs. Doyle returned to clear the plates.

"Everything was delicious," Shane told her, before tossing his napkin onto his plate and passing it to her.

"I'm glad you all liked it." She pointed to my plate, the only one with food still remaining. "Was everything okay with yours, dear? Would you like me to make you anything else?"

"No, no. It was great. I had a big lunch and don't have much of an appetite." I waved off her concern, handing over my plate.

"Well, I hope you made room for dessert," Penn said, standing from the table.

"Oh, I couldn't." I patted my stomach, shaking my head. "But I'd love to hear more about you two. I feel like all we've done is talk about ourselves to—" Before I could finish the sentence, Penn was out of the room, following Mrs. Doyle into the kitchen.

"Mrs. Doyle makes the best chocolate cake," Etta said, as if I hadn't spoken at all. I looked over at Leo, hoping he'd back me up. He met my eye, then shrugged one shoulder as if to say, *let's not make a scene.*

"It sounds great," Piper said, her gaze dancing around the table, not lingering on me for too long. Had I just made things awkward for everyone? I sighed, sinking farther into my chair as I tried to figure out how to bring it up again.

Why were they being so shady? Why wouldn't they tell us anything about themselves? Was I just being paranoid? I really didn't think so.

I looked over at Lakynn, whose eyes widened slightly at me as Henry continued chatting with Etta. How was he able to carry on a conversation so easily? I'd never understood it.

Upon seeing Lakynn's worried expression though, I finally knew I wasn't alone in my concerns, even if I was the most vocal. Was I just on edge because of the scream we'd heard earlier? Maybe, but I didn't feel like that was entirely it.

I'd had this nagging sense of dread all evening, and it was further cemented by the odd way our hosts were acting.

"Anyway, it's one of the best films. You'll have to check it out. I think it's on Netflix, but it might be Hulu. You have both, don't you?" Henry was asking.

"Of course," Etta said, looking every bit as intrigued with him as he seemed with her.

"Everyone has everything now," Leo said, a bit too loudly, causing everyone from the head of the table to look in our direction. He paused, seeming shocked that everyone had looked at him. "I-I mean, you know, there are like... dozens of platforms. We're all paying more now for all the streamers than we were for cable. So much for cutting the cord." He chuckled.

Shane nodded in agreement, as if it were the most original thought in the world. "You're so right. And, as soon as you decide to cancel one, they come out with something you want to see and reel you back in."

There was a hum of laughter just as Penn and Mrs.

Doyle reappeared in the doorway, each with two plates of chocolate cake in their hands.

The warm scent of the cake hit my nose the instant they were in the room, making my stomach grumble involuntarily. I'd never been much of a meat eater, but sweets were my weakness, despite the assumptions based on my career.

They placed the plates down in front of Etta, Henry, Shane, and Piper, then made their way back out of the room quickly.

"Hey, Henry, I forgot to ask how everything went the other day. With that customer you were having trouble with," Piper said. Her tone was casual and she wasn't meeting his eye, but I sensed there was something more to her question.

"What customer?" Lakynn asked.

"Oh, it was nothing," Henry assured her. "Just a customer who got mad when I couldn't refill a prescription early. Piper just happened to stop by the store in time to hear me get cussed out." If Piper's question had worried me, Henry's answer put me at ease. There was no stress in his voice or the way he held himself. If anything, he was cheerfully sarcastic about the entire thing.

"It was awful," Piper said, cutting off a piece of her cake. She made no move to take a bite.

"You didn't tell me about that," Lakynn said softly, concern etched on her face.

"Come on, a rude customer?" Leo said loudly. "Just another Thursday, am I right? I'm lucky if I only get cussed out twelve times a day anymore. You guys don't know how good you've got it not having to work directly with the public."

"Uh, we all *do* work with the public, Leo," I said, nodding my head.

"Yeah, well, not Lakynn or Shane. And you, if you have a shitty customer, you can just *not* fix their teeth. Or Piper can *not* do their accounting or whatever. Me and Henry just have to grin and bear it. Or, in my case, flip 'em off through the phone and bear it."

Henry patted the table. "He's right. It was no big deal, honestly. Just par for the course." He patted Lakynn's hand gently, his touch lingering on her skin. "I swear it's fine."

"Were you sick?" Shane asked Piper, his voice low.

She shook her head, still staring at her untouched cake. "No, just...um, just..." She paused, catching her breath, and when she looked up, her expression was unreadable. She furrowed her brows. "Sorry, what did you say?"

"I asked if you were sick, when you went to the pharmacy. You should've told me. I would've gone for you."

"I wasn't sick," she said, though she didn't get to elaborate further, because at that moment, the door opened again and Penn and Mrs. Doyle were back with the remaining plates.

They set them down in front of the rest of us, the last plate going in front of Penn, and Mrs. Doyle surveyed the room, checking that everyone had a plate.

"Well, then, everything is washed and put away except for those plates. I've wrapped the leftovers. So, I'll be heading home if that's all you need from me tonight," she said.

A boulder of dread filled my stomach at the possibility of her leaving. I didn't know why—I had no more reason to trust her than I did Penn and Etta, but somehow, the idea of her leaving the house, leaving us here alone with them, was enough to bring back the worry I'd been doing my best to quash.

I picked up my fork, deciding I'd had enough of whatever this night was supposed to be. If they wouldn't tell us any more about themselves, I was done answering their questions. To avoid being rude, I'd eat a few bites of the cake and then insist we leave. I'd drag Leo with me if I had to, and I sensed Lakynn would get on board with the plan without much coercion.

As my fork cut through the cake for the first time, I froze. Ice-cold fear ricocheted through my chest, taking hold of my organs.

I moved more of the chocolate dessert, trying to make sense of what I was seeing, but it was impossible.

I glanced up at the rest of the table, checking to see if they'd noticed my panic, but to my relief, no one had.

I moved the last bit of cake until I could see the final piece of the note tucked under my dessert.

Someone has been lying to you.

CHAPTER TWELVE

PIPER

All around me, the table buzzed with quiet conversation. Leo was chatting with Shane about some new video game and Etta had just asked Lakynn more about her company.

I was thankful that, for everyone else, life seemed to be moving on at a normal pace, because I'd been practically frozen in fear from the moment I cut into my cake.

I stared at the note that had been hidden under the warm, gooey chocolate dessert, visible only once I'd sliced into it.

Someone knows your secret.

What did it mean?

Who knew my secret?

What secret were they even talking about?

Who put this note on my plate?

I stared at it, blinking in what felt like slow motion, then glanced back up, trying to steady my breathing. I shoved the cake back into place to cover the message, appetite lost, and pushed the cake away from me.

"Everything okay, Piper?" Penn asked.

Was there something sinister in his eyes? Or was I imagining it? Mrs. Doyle had been the one to deliver my plate. Was she trying to send me a message?

Suddenly, everyone was a suspect as I stared around the table. Was this a joke? Was this some sort of prank that everyone was in on?

Once, I'd at least had Allen who I would've been able to trust. If he were here, I'd be able to search his face for a hint of laughter or trickery. Now, though, I was alone. If they were pranking me for some reason, the couples all had their person to rely on, which only left Shane and me. But, as much as I liked and trusted Shane, I didn't know him well enough to know if the tension in his neck was a sign that something was wrong or just that he was particularly tired. He wasn't my husband.

As I had so many other times since Allen left, I found myself feeling completely and utterly alone.

"Piper?" Penn asked again, reminding me I still hadn't answered him.

"Sorry—yes," I blurted out. "I, um, I'm not sure I have room for dessert, after all."

"Everything okay?" Bethany asked, pulling my attention to her.

I nodded, meeting her eyes. "I'm fine. Just tired. I think I'm going to go home, actually." I waited for them to tell me this was all a joke, or for laughter to ring out, but it didn't. Instead, there was a pause, my words hanging in the air, and then everyone seemed to release a collective breath.

"I'll walk you home," Shane said.

"You don't have to—"

"We'll come, too." That was Bethany, already out of her seat. Had I misread things? Now, everyone seemed all too eager to get out of there.

"Oh, no. I hate to see you all leaving so soon," Etta said, watching as we rose from our chairs and pushed them back up to the table. To my surprise, she didn't stand or try to stop us. Maybe I'd misread everything, after all.

"It's getting late," Bethany said. "We need to check on the kids before bed anyway."

Releasing a loud yawn, Lakynn nodded, standing up as Bethany tugged Leo to his feet.

"We should get going, too," Lakynn said. "But dinner was delicious, and this cake was divine. If I'd known it was coming, I would've saved more room." She patted her stomach. "Seriously, thank you. And welcome to the neighborhood. Dinner at our place next, okay?" She looked down at Henry, who was shuffling around the last bit of cake on his plate. Begrudgingly, he stood, dabbing his lips with the cloth napkin in front of him before placing it over his plate.

He looked as though he were going to argue with Lakynn but thought better of it. "Well," he said with a sigh, "I guess she's right. We should say good night. I hate to eat and run, but,"—he checked his watch—"if we don't get the dog let out soon, she'll be mad at us."

"I understand," Penn said, as he and Etta rose to their feet finally. "We're so glad you all could join us tonight. I hope everything was to your liking."

Our echo chamber of praise was instantaneous:

"It was delicious."

"So good."

"Thank you for the invitation."

"The best meal I've had in a long time."

"This was great. You'll have to give me the recipe."

"I can't wait for next time."

Henry held out a hand to shake Penn's while Lakynn pulled Etta into a quick hug. We made our way around, saying brief goodbyes and thanking them again for their hospitality. I glanced over my shoulder just one more time, waving at our hosts over my shoulder as we made our way as a group toward the exit.

Etta and Penn stood by the table, his arm around her waist, small smiles on their faces as we disappeared around the corner. It felt strange that they weren't following us to see us out, but I was too relieved to be away from them to care. I just wanted to get out of that house.

"Well, that was odd," Henry whispered heatedly.

"What was?" Lakynn whispered back.

"The dinner. You didn't think so?"

"Everything okay?" Leo asked Bethany.

"I was just ready to leave," she said.

"*I* thought it was odd, yes. I didn't realize *you* did," Lakynn said as we neared the front door. We all checked behind us every few steps, making sure we weren't being followed.

"What's that supposed to mean?" Henry asked, elbowing her playfully.

"You seemed like you were having a great time, that's all."

"I just didn't want to be rude," he said plainly.

"I wasn't rude."

"I never said you—"

"Everyone else was leaving. I didn't want to walk home alone in the dark," Lakynn said quickly.

"Walking with me would've been walking alone?"

"You know what I mean!" she whisper-shouted.

Shane and I were in the back, and he glanced at me once, a playful smirk on his lips as if to say, *Hey, at least we don't sound like that.*

Lakynn reached the door first, stretching her hand out for the doorknob as we all stopped just behind her. She twisted the knob and Henry reached out, ready to pull the door open for us all, but the door didn't budge. She twisted it again, this time more frantically, then reached up and ran her hand over the lock, which required a key to turn.

"What's wrong?" Henry asked, nudging her out of the way to turn the knob himself. She didn't answer, but she didn't need to. We all understood without either of them saying a single word. I checked behind me, panic filling my stomach as I waited for Penn and Etta to emerge from around the corner, trapping us in the narrow hallway.

"It's locked," Henry said after a moment, the incessant rattle of the doorknob ceasing. "We're locked in."

"Wait, what?" Leo asked, stepping forward for his own turn at trying to pull it open.

"It has to be a mistake," Shane said.

"Maybe it just sticks," Bethany agreed, searching behind her. "Why didn't they walk us to the door?"

No one seemed to have an answer. Suddenly, everyone was shoving forward, reaching for the door and the doorknob as we tried to pry it open. I could practically smell the fear then—if fear has a smell.

Sweat and panic permeated the air and then, all at once, we stopped, taking in the sight of each other.

"There's probably an explanation," Henry said, his tone unconvincing. I reached for the door to the study next to me. It was probably dramatic, but I wanted to check the windows to see if we could escape through those if necessary.

"This is locked, too," I said, placing a hand on the only door in the hall.

"What the hell is going on?" Leo asked, moving toward me and trying the door for himself. Suddenly, the too-white walls surrounding us felt as if they were closing in. Henry smacked the door with a loud CRACK, causing us all to shriek.

"Jesus," Lakynn complained, as the sound echoed through the hall. "Don't break it."

"It has to be stuck." He swiped a hand across his forehead, then dried his palm on his pants.

"We'll just go ask them. Maybe there's a trick to it," Shane said calmly, jutting his head back in the direction of the kitchen.

I glanced down the hall again, wondering if it was possible they hadn't heard us struggling to get out. Maybe Shane was right. Maybe our panic was premature. There were six of us, after all, and just two of them. If they meant to do us harm, they could've poisoned us. But no one seemed to be feeling ill.

Maybe the message on my plate was just a prank after all, but I couldn't shake the fear in my gut. Suddenly, everything was a message, a warning, a whisper of imminent danger.

"Come on," Henry said, nodding as if trying to convince himself. I held my breath as we retreated back toward the kitchen, still trying to concoct a reasonable explanation as to why we couldn't get the door open.

As we passed through the kitchen and rounded the corner to step back into the dining room, the terror overcame me, the hairs on the back of my neck standing at attention.

"Etta? Penn?" Henry called as we stared around the empty room.

Bethany met my eyes, and I saw my panic reflected back to me.

Henry paced the room, looking here and there—back and forth, back and forth, back and forth—the floorboards creaking with each step. More sweat beaded on his forehead as he stopped in his tracks and turned to face us, putting into words what we could plainly see. "They're...gone."

CHAPTER THIRTEEN

LAKYNN

"Where could they have gone?" I asked my husband as we all spread out, checking reasonable places—the kitchen, the hall again, the living room—and less-than-reasonable places—under the table, behind the curtains, inside the kitchen cabinets.

"I have no idea. *Penn, Etta!*" he called, hands cupped around his mouth. "Where are you guys?"

Shane, Leo, and Bethany returned from the living room, breathless and wide eyed.

"They aren't in there," Bethany said, her eyes locked with mine. "And all the doors in the hall are locked."

"What about the door off of the kitchen?" I asked, trying to recall if we'd checked that already. Everything was starting to blur together. "Or...the one in the hallway that leads to the patio?"

"I checked it," Bethany said.

"The kitchen door, too. I'm sure we checked it," Henry said, though he turned and walked out of the room, and moments later I heard the banging sound of him pulling on the door once again.

"It's like they vanished," Leo agreed.

"Okay, well, they can't have vanished," Henry said plainly when he reappeared, out of breath. "They're around here somewhere. Maybe they're upstairs. Did you check there?"

"We can't get upstairs," Bethany said. "The door to the stairwell is locked. Everything's locked."

"Okay, so that's probably where they are, then. Sound doesn't carry well here, with the concrete walls. They probably just can't hear us." I could tell he didn't believe his own explanation.

"You seriously think they don't hear us down here screaming? And, even if they don't, why didn't they clean up? All of our plates are still here," Piper said, moving around the table to examine her own plate. "And why are all the doors locked anyway?"

"This place is locked down like Fort Knox," Leo said. "I'll bet they lock up the toilet paper."

"None of that matters," Bethany said sharply. "Who cares where they are? Why are we locked in? That's all that matters. Why are we locked in and how the hell do we get out?"

"Check the windows," Piper said. "Maybe we can get out of a window. The study is locked, but what about those?" She pointed to a window on the far wall covered by a long, golden curtain. We moved toward it in a scramble, but Piper reached it first, pulling it back with a single, quick motion.

She gasped, then placed a hand on the pane before looking back at us.

Of course.

The window was barred over, making it impossible to smash through in hopes of escape. It was another security measure we'd seen them install.

We were trapped here.

Rats in a cage.

"Check the others," Henry instructed, pointing this way and that. Everyone scattered, setting into action, scurrying around as if to further prove ourselves rodents. "Maybe there's one somewhere that they didn't bar up."

I think, even then, we were trying to remain calm, trying to rationalize everything when there was nothing rational about what was happening.

There was nothing that explained the locked doors or the barred windows. Nothing that explained the sudden disappearance of our hosts. Sickness and fear crashed into me like waves, ebbing and flowing with each passing moment. The sensation was dizzying—I was either going to vomit or pass out.

"Etta! Penn! Guys, where did you go?" Leo shouted from another room.

I heard the banging sound of someone in our group trying to bust down a door somewhere, bringing me back to reality. I needed to figure a way out of this. Needed to get everyone on the same page. Working toward a solution.

If I didn't, more chaos would follow.

It was up to me.

"Everyone, calm down!" I directed, snapping into action and pulling my phone from the pocket of my dress. "Let's just call for help. It's the simplest solution."

"Who will we call? The kids? They're not home and

they don't have a key. What good will that do besides to freak them out?" Henry asked.

I thought for a moment. "Okay, so we'll call the police."

"The police?" He said it with a scoff, obviously thinking the suggestion was ridiculous. He didn't realize how much danger we were in.

No one did.

Not yet, anyway.

"Yes, the police. We're trapped in here with no way out."

Everyone in the room seemed to inhale in unison. I opened the browser, trying to search for the nonemergency number. Even I wasn't quite sure it was an emergency just yet. The page was white, loading slowly, the progress bar across the top at a standstill.

"I don't have service..." I said breathlessly, shaking my head.

"*Shit*. It's the concrete walls and metal roof," Henry said, glancing up. "Remember? It was why Tom and Eleanor had the landline."

"Just dial 9-1-1," Piper said stiffly. "It'll go through no matter what."

"No," Shane corrected. "Not if there's no service."

"Yes. Even if there's no service, 9-1-1 is still supposed to work," Bethany argued.

"You're correct, but the idea is wrong. If your cell phone provider doesn't have service, a 9-1-1 call will still connect to any tower it can, but if there's no service at all, it's not going to go through." He nodded toward me. "But, I mean, try it. Just in case."

"How do you know so much about this?" Bethany asked, her tone accusatory.

"I'm a writer," Shane answered as I dialed the numbers, my hands shaking. "I'm a wealth of useless knowledge."

Bethany mumbled something under her breath that sounded like "convenient." I put the phone to my ear, waiting...

Waiting...

Waiting...

Cursing, I put the phone down and ended the call. "He's right."

"Can you get service if you stand by a window?" Henry asked, pointing to the nearest one.

I moved toward it, shaking my head. "No. Nothing."

"Let me try." Leo pulled out his phone, tapping the numbers in angrily.

"This has to be a prank, right?" Henry asked with a soft laugh. "I mean, what the hell is going on?"

"We need to look around. They have to be here somewhere," Shane said.

"We should try to break down the door," Piper said.

"No, the only thing that will do is get someone hurt. I agree with Shane," said Henry. "Let's look around. There's gotta be an explanation. Or, at the very least, another way out."

"Is there a back door somewhere?" Shane asked, looking at me. "You mentioned a door to the patio?"

"Third door on the right," I said, pointing down the hall. "It leads to the laundry room and then out to the pool area, but Bethany said she already checked it." I looked to her for confirmation.

She nodded. "Every single door in the hall is locked. I triple-checked them all."

"What about the landline you mentioned?" Shane asked Henry. "Where is it? Maybe it's still here."

"It was right there," Henry said, pointing to the wall where the phone had once been mounted. "And I think they kept one somewhere upstairs, but if that one's gone, I'm not sure Penn and Etta would've kept the other."

Shane cursed under his breath. "Okay, what then? We're just trapped here?"

"Let's not panic," I said.

Henry nodded. "She's right. We'll..." He ran a hand over his mouth, releasing a puff of air. "Okay, let's just look around again and double-check the doors. Maybe we're missing something."

Piper opened her mouth to protest, but Henry was quick to interrupt her.

"It's not the best option, but it's the only one we've got right now. Unless you have something better in mind."

She closed her mouth. Out of options, no one else bothered to argue. We moved together, searching for clues on the whereabouts of our mysterious hosts. Occasionally, I checked my phone signal to see if it had improved, but the notification at the top of my screen let me know I still had no service.

"What's that?" Bethany asked, interrupting my wandering thoughts. She darted across the kitchen, finger outstretched toward something stuck to the front of the refrigerator. It was the only thing attached to the stainless steel appliance. A small scrap of white paper held in place by a round, blue magnet. "Was this here before?"

Shane and Leo shrugged.

"What's it say?" Henry asked.

We moved closer to her as she read it over. "It's a...poem? Or a quote?"

"Read it," I prompted, stepping behind her to try to make out the scratchy handwriting.

"The more of me there is, the less you see," she read aloud.

"What does that mean?" Leo asked.

"It's probably not for us," Piper said.

"I swear it wasn't here before, though," Bethany mused.

"Is it a riddle?" Shane asked. He held out his hand, taking the paper and reading over it once more. "The more of me there is, the less you see..."

"Sounds like a dumb advertisement, if you ask me," Leo said, groaning.

"Maybe it's a private note. We should put it back," Henry said.

"The more of me, the less you see..." I whispered, trying to think. "Why would I see less?"

"You think he's right?" Bethany asked, glancing toward Shane. "It's a riddle?"

"No," I said, shaking my head. "I mean, I don't know, but what else do we have to go on?"

"It doesn't make any sense. We should keep looking around for a way out. This is a waste of time. It's getting late," Henry said.

I nodded slowly, but as I did, Piper gasped.

"What is it?" I asked.

"Something he said..." She narrowed her gaze, lost in thought.

"What?" I pried, hoping she'd found a way—any way—to get us out.

"The more of me there is, the less you see..." Her eyes widened. "Shane's right. It's a riddle. And the answer—I think it's... Could it be *darkness?*"

She met my eyes with hope filling her expression.

Then, as if in answer to her question, the house went dark.

CHAPTER FOURTEEN

BETHANY

S *hit.*
    Shit.
Shit.
Shit.
Shit.

I darted across the dark room, bumping into people and objects in my path and screaming every time.

They're going to kill us.

They've got us in the dark and they're going to kill us. We're not going to see it coming. We're not going to know who's next.

I replayed every horror movie I'd ever watched in my head, waiting to feel an arm slip around my neck or a blade slice my skin. If I just kept moving, they couldn't catch me.

"Everyone, stop!" Lakynn shouted over the commotion. "Panicking isn't going to help anyone. We need to be calm. Rational."

The sound of the scattered footprints slowed, halting finally.

I couldn't see anything in the pitch-black room, but I turned toward the sound of her voice once I could hear it more clearly.

A single light shone through the darkness.

A phone.

Lakynn held her phone up, blinding us with the brightness as if we were teens who'd snuck into an R-rated movie being caught by the security guard.

If only there were a security guard here...

"I know this is scary," she said, nodding slowly. "I'm scared, too. But we're not helpless. The lights are out and that sucks, but we have flashlights in our pockets. Everyone get your phones out and give us as much light as possible."

We did as she instructed. I think I was just so glad someone was telling me what to do when all I wanted to do was melt into the ground, a puddle of panic.

Once there were six beams of light shining through the room, it seemed a little less terrifying.

"What are we going to do?" Henry asked, stepping up next to Lakynn.

"I'm not sure yet," she admitted. "But we should stick together. Whatever's going on, I have to believe we're safer together."

"Unless one of us is behind this." I heard Piper's voice from across the room and spun around, trying to track her down with my beam of light.

Soon, most of the light in the room was directed toward her. "What do you mean?" Lakynn asked.

"Nothing," she said, holding a hand up to shield her eyes. "Just thinking out loud."

"If you have something to say, you should say it," Henry said, almost aggressively. It was rare to hear him be anything but friendly.

"Just forget it," she said. "We should look around, try to find Etta and Penn or...a breaker box or a window without bars. We have to find a way out of here. Or maybe the landline phone, like Shane said."

"I agree." When Lakynn spoke, we turned the lights back toward her. "We'll go down the hall as a group and see what we can find." Without waiting for anyone to agree or giving anyone the chance to protest, she turned, leading the way across the kitchen and toward the hall. Our beams of light followed her, the group huddled close together as we moved in unison.

Someone bumped into my side, and I jolted, turning the light to get a clear picture of who it was.

"Piper?"

She nodded, shielding her eyes. "Everything okay with you?"

I turned the light away from her, jogging to keep up with the group as we entered the hallway.

"You mean aside from the obvious?"

"Yeah, I guess so," she murmured.

"I'm just scared... And confused. What about you?"

We stopped at the first set of doors. Half the group turned to the left and the rest of us turned to the right, attempting to open one of the two doors.

"This one's locked," Henry confirmed.

"This one, too," Shane said.

"Can I talk to you?" a voice whispered in the darkness, too close to my ear. I jumped, though I knew it was her, and spun around, flashing the light in her direction just to be sure.

"Um, sure, what's up?"

Piper's light flashed across my face, then back down to our feet as the others moved on to the next door. "There was a weird message on my plate at dinner."

My stomach knotted. I'd practically forgotten about the note hidden under my cake in all the chaos. Was it possible that Piper had gotten a similar one? "What kind of weird message?"

"It said—"

"This one's definitely locked, too." A light shone in our direction. "Keep up, you two!" Henry commanded, and I realized we'd fallen too far behind.

We moved forward as I waited for her answer. "It said that someone knows my secret."

My pulse quickened, my throat suddenly too dry. "Your secret?"

"Yeah."

"What secret?"

"I have no idea. All I can think of is...well, you know."

"It's not that. It can't be." I dismissed her concern. We were quiet for a moment as the group stopped at the next set of doors. Finally, I said, "I got one, too."

"What? A note? You did? Did yours say the same thing?"

"Not exactly. It said..." I thought back to the note, the memory sending chills across the nape of my neck. "It said that someone has been lying to me."

"Lying?" she asked, and I fought the urge to shine the

97

light in her face again. I wanted to see her expression, if only to reassure me it was as strange as I thought. That I wasn't overreacting. My mind seemed to be at war with what made sense and the reality of what was happening. "About what?"

"I have no idea. But I doubt it's about anything to do with...*that*."

"Do you think this is all connected?"

"What all?"

"The notes. Being locked in here. The darkness. It's like someone's pulling a big, elaborate prank."

"Maybe," I said, "but I don't think it's any of us. Everyone seems really scared."

I felt her hand on my arm. "Do you think the others got notes, too?"

"I don't know, really. Should we ask them?"

"Ask us what?" I jolted as a new voice spoke from directly beside me.

Lakynn.

"Jesus." I put a hand on my chest, trying to catch my breath.

"Did I scare you?" she asked, shining the light under her own face, so there were shadows across her features. She looked as if she were preparing to tell us a ghost story around a campfire. "I saw you two back here talking...wanted to make sure everything was okay."

"They're all locked," Shane said, cursing under his breath.

"*Fuck.*" One of the men—Henry, I thought, but I couldn't be sure—slapped a door, the sound reverberating through the hall.

"Okay. Let's go back toward the kitchen. At least we can

pull back the curtains and get a little light in here that way," Henry said eventually, though I was skeptical. He was right earlier. It was getting late. The darkness had settled in outside. According to my phone, it was already after nine. With no streetlights in our cul-de-sac, I very much doubted there'd be enough light outside to do more than our phones were currently doing. Either way, I was glad to be out of the long, narrow hallway, with too many doors and too many places to hide.

"We're okay," Piper said, answering the question I'd practically forgotten Lakynn had asked. "How about you?"

"I'm starting to get worried," she admitted. "There's enough of us in here, if things get really bad, if people start getting too scared, I'm worried someone will get seriously hurt. Or worse. I'm just trying to keep everyone calm, even if that feels impossible."

"What do you think is going on?" Piper asked. "Really."

"I have no idea," Lakynn said. "I think that's the worst part. Not knowing whether we're *under-* or *over*reacting."

"Hey, did you get a note at dinner?" I asked, blurting out the question before I'd had time to figure out how to bring it up.

"A note?" Lakynn asked. "What do you mean?"

"Under your cake," Piper said. "That's where mine was."

"Mine too."

Lakynn was quiet for a moment. "I'm confused."

"You mean you didn't get one?"

We were back in the kitchen then, and Shane, Leo, and Henry were opening the curtains for the four windows in the room, allowing a bit more light in. It didn't make a world of difference, but at least now I could make out the vague outlines of everyone when they moved near a window. Or maybe my eyes were just beginning to adjust to the darkness.

"What kind of note?" Lakynn asked.

"Mine said someone's been lying to me, and Piper's said someone knows her secret. We aren't sure what to make of them, but we assumed everyone got one since we both did."

"Well, I didn't," Lakynn said softly. "I wonder what they mean. And who sent them?"

"We have no idea," Piper said. "Mrs. Doyle, maybe? Or Penn? But, as for the why, I'm as lost as you are."

"We also thought, well, we thought maybe it was one of us. Like a prank or something," I added.

"This has to all be connected somehow. They're telling us something," Lakynn said.

"Who is?" Piper asked.

"Whoever's doing this."

"I just don't understand why you didn't get one. Why just me and Bethany?"

Lakynn sighed. "I have no idea. This is all so confusing."

"Okay, with all the doors locked in both hallways—" I could see Henry's hand moving in the direction of the entrance hall, then down the hall where the bedrooms were. "That leaves us only having access to the living room, dining room, and kitchen. So we need to split up and check all the windows and rooms again, just in case. I know we're grasping at straws here, people, but it's better than sitting around and doing nothing. Lakynn, you help me check things out in here, Piper and Shane can go together to the living room, and Leo and Bethany can check the dining room. Try to open any window you can. Search for anything that might help us. Check your phones periodically for a signal. Let's meet back here in, like, twenty minutes. And, whatever you do, don't leave your partner alone."

Everyone whipped their flashlights around, beams scanning the room as we each looked for our partners. The scent of Leo's cologne hit me before I saw him, but as I felt a hand on the small of my back, a sense of calm washed over me.

Even in the darkness, my husband always made me feel safe.

"What do you think's going on?" he asked when we'd separated from the group.

"I have no idea," I admitted as he pulled me into the dining room. "Hey, did you have a note on your plate at dinner?"

"A note? What kind of note?" We froze in place, and I felt him turn to face me.

"Piper and I both got one." I told him about the notes quickly, relaying what they'd said. "But Lakynn says she didn't have one."

"I didn't either," he said, clicking his tongue. "What do you think they mean?"

"I have no idea," I said softly. "But it's really freaking me out."

He ran a hand over my arm in the darkness, the hand holding his phone dropping down to his side. "Hey, you know I'm not going to let anything happen to you, right?"

I gave a small smile, though he couldn't see it. "Oh, you're my knight in shining armor, are you?"

"You know it." His lips pressed to my skin in what felt like an attempt to kiss my forehead, but instead, in the darkness, he landed awkwardly on my eyelid.

When he pulled back, I sighed. "I'm not sure why Henry

wanted us to come in here. We've already checked this window and this room. The phone's not in here, the window's barred over, and the room's basically empty, remember?"

He gave my arm a gentle squeeze. "I know, but Henry's right. Anything is better than nothing right now. Let's just see if we can open the window again. Even just an inch or two. Maybe if we can, we can signal someone for help."

"Through the solid concrete wall? Who would see us?"

"Maybe Mrs. Morgan would hear us," he said, and even in the moonlight his shrug was obviously halfhearted. We were grasping at straws and we both knew it. Even if, by chance, Mrs. Morgan was awake and outside of her house at nearly ten o'clock at night, I doubted very much that she'd be able to hear our screams from this far away.

Either way, I was too exhausted to argue. Instead, I nodded, gripping his hand as he pulled me across the room. He tugged at the window, groaning and grunting as he attempted to pull it up, but it didn't budge.

"Nope. No. It won't open." He panted, swiping the back of his hand across his forehead. "It's like they're all nailed shut." From where we stood, I could just barely make out the worry etched in his expression.

"What are we going to do, Leo? We have to get home to our kids. We have to." Images of the kids coming home and searching the house for us with no hope of finding us flooded through my mind, making my chest ache so terribly I could hardly catch my breath. "They need us." I wanted that to be true. Needed it to be true.

"We're going to be okay. Do you hear me?" He gripped both my shoulders, his phone digging into my arm. "We're going to get out of here. We just have to stick together and figure out what it is they want from us."

"You mean Etta and Penn? You really think they're behind this?"

"Yeah, who else?" He nodded, staring off as if lost in thought.

"What?" I prompted.

"I was just thinking... I think Mrs. Doyle must be involved somehow, too. She's the only one who could've locked the doors after we came in. Penn only left us once, and he wasn't gone long enough to have locked everything up. But Mrs. Doyle had all the time when we were eating."

"That would make sense. Maybe they were working together somehow. Maybe she and Penn put the notes on our plates."

"Plates," he said, eyes wide. "That's right. We should check the plates. See if we can figure out who else had a note."

"Good idea. We're running out of time," I said, making my way toward the table quickly. "Hurry." I checked Lakynn's plate first, shoving her cake onto the tablecloth without care. To both my surprise and relief, it was empty, just like she'd said. I didn't want to doubt my best friend, but this place had me questioning everyone.

I moved to my plate next, wanting to see if my note was still there. I shoved the cake out of the way, shining the flashlight over the plate.

"Mine's still here." I lifted it off the plate, waving the chocolate-smeared paper in the air. He shined the light at me, squinting as he tried to read it, then lowered the light. "Lakynn really didn't have one."

"You thought she was lying?" he asked. His light was shining over Shane's plate as he shoved the cake to the side.

"I don't know. I don't know what to believe right now. Are you telling me you don't suspect that someone here might be involved?"

Truth be told, I wasn't sure what to believe anymore.

"These are our friends, Beth. We can't forget that. That's what they want us to do." He swiped his hand on a napkin. "Shane's plate's empty. No note."

"How are you so levelheaded right now?" I shined my light at him, watching as he moved onto Piper's plate.

"I'm just—"

A sound from across the room cut him off, and we both froze.

Buzz.

Buzz.

Buzz.

CHAPTER FIFTEEN

PIPER

"Guys, come here! We found something!" I heard Bethany's cries echo through the house and spun around to where I could hear Shane noisily trying to open one of the windows in the living room. He stopped short, both of us staring at each other for just a moment, processing what we'd heard. Then, all at once, we took off, darting across the room and toward the dining room.

"What is it? What'd you find?" Henry asked, he and Lakynn just seconds ahead of us.

"Shh!" Bethany said, a hand out in the blinding light from our phones. "Listen. We can't figure out where it's coming from."

The room grew still and quiet.

For a second, I didn't hear anything at all. Then...

Buzz.

Buzz.

Buzz.

"It's coming from over here somewhere," Bethany said, pointing toward the far wall.

"Or maybe the floor." I moved my light toward the voice and spotted Leo finally, lying down on the dining room floor, an ear to the ground. "I can't tell."

"It sounds like a phone," Henry whispered. Lakynn followed his movements like a spotlight with her phone as he jogged across the room and placed an ear to the wall. After a moment, he pulled away, squinting his eyes long enough to look into the bright light and nod. "Bethany's right. It's coming from the wall."

"What room is on the other side?" Lakynn asked.

"A bedroom, probably. Whatever it is, we don't have access to it."

Leo sat up from the floor, dusting his hands. "We have to have access. There's gotta be something we're missing here."

"Like what?" I asked.

"How do you know?" Bethany asked at the same time.

"Because it's...it's like a game. First the riddle, now this." He sighed. "Look, I'm not going to pretend to have a clue what's going on, but if there's one thing I understand, it's games. And this is playing out just like a game. We need to find the source of the buzzing, and I'm betting you anything it'll point us in the direction of another clue."

"But this isn't a game, Leo," I said gently. "It's real life. We're really here."

"I think he's right," Shane said, and I flicked my light in the direction of his voice. "The riddle was our first clue. Maybe this is just all some sort of game."

"Well, I quit." Bethany's hands were up when a beam of

light hit her. "I quit. I forfeit. You all win. I just want to go home. I don't want to play whatever the hell this is."

We were silent for a moment, as if waiting for the lights to come on and the game to end. As if waiting for Penn to walk out like he were hosting a game show to tell us what we'd lost.

Then...

Buzz.

Buzz.

Buzz.

Bethany's hands dropped dramatically. "I hate this," she whined.

"Hang on," Leo said. His light was directed at the far wall.

An air vent.

He dropped to his knees in front of it, shining his light through the narrow slats.

Buzz.

Buzz.

Buzz.

"It's coming from in here." He slapped his palm on the outside of the air vent dramatically, a proud smile on his face.

"What is it?" Shane asked.

"I don't know. I can see something, but I can't tell what it is." He tugged on the cover, but it didn't budge. He leaned closer, using his flashlight to illuminate the corners of the vent. "Does anyone happen to have a screwdriver?"

"Quick! Check the kitchen drawers!" Henry said, and I heard a scuffle of feet headed in that direction.

I thought about what Leo had said. Was this really some

sort of game? And, if so, what was the prize? Was it all just in good fun? If so, some warning and permission were necessary. Like Bethany, I had no time or interest in playing games. I wanted to go home to check on Dudley, my cat, and curl up in bed.

"What about this?" I heard Bethany ask, interrupting my thoughts. When I looked up, she was holding a butter knife in the air, pointed toward her husband. "Will that work?"

He slipped it from her hand and placed the knife between the grooves of the screw. "Keep the light on me." He placed his phone down, using both hands to turn the knife slowly, the screw hardly budging.

After a few painful moments, I heard footsteps headed in our direction.

"We didn't find anything," Lakynn said, panting and out of breath.

"It's okay, I think this is working," Leo said, just as the screw slipped for the first time, easing forward just barely. We watched with breathless anticipation as he turned the knife inch by inch, one hand over the other. Once he had it loosened enough, he grabbed hold of it with his finger and twisted it the rest of the way out, then moved on to the next corner.

Several painstaking minutes later, all four screws had been removed and Leo looked back at us once, nodding apprehensively before turning his attention back to the vent.

"Be careful," Bethany warned.

He grabbed hold of both sides, preparing to pull it free.

Buzz.

Buzz.

Buzz.

Buzz.

With a single swift motion, he tugged the vent free, sending dust in every direction. I coughed, fanning my face as I tried to see what was inside.

"What the..." He leaned in, reaching toward whatever it was. "What the hell is this?"

CHAPTER SIXTEEN

LAKYNN

L eo lifted the object into the beams of light so we could get a better look.

He lifted *two* objects, actually.

One was an alarm clock, which had been the source of all the buzzing. The other was long, metal, and black. It took me an extra second to recognize it, but when he turned it over so I could see one end, I knew.

"Is it some sort of flashlight?" Bethany asked.

"I think s—" He clicked the opposite end and a violet light shone through the room. "Not a flashlight. A *black* light," he said, too much excitement in his voice.

"What for? So we can see where they killed their last victims?" Piper asked dryly.

"Don't talk like that," Henry said. He placed a protective hand on my back.

"Why not? We obviously know something is really, really wrong here—"

"Guys, look!" Leo shouted, drawing our attention to the opposite wall.

I spun around, following the single beam of violet light to the wall above the dining table. The clue had been hidden there all along—all through the meal, all through the evening.

Waiting for us to find it.

How long had they been planning this?

"Trek or saunter, patrol or wander, underfoot you'll find me. Whether a bad day or a hard night, with the remedy I'll be rhyming," Leo read aloud, moving the violet light along the wall as he revealed each new word. "That's it. That's all it says."

"What the hell does that mean?" Shane asked with a groan.

"It's another riddle," Bethany said.

"With the remedy I'll be rhyming... The remedy... What is the remedy for a bad day?" Leo asked, snapping his fingers as he thought aloud.

"Jesus, I don't know, a fucking drink?" Shane said, groaning loudly. "That's what I need at this point." He fanned himself with his shirt. "Is anyone else hot? It's gotta be like ninety in here."

He was right. As he said it, I was currently blowing air from my lips in an attempt to dry the sweat on my chin.

"You don't walk on a drink," Henry said, sticking to the task at hand.

"No, you don't have to..." Leo said, obviously getting frustrated with us. "That's not the point. Read it again." He whipped the beam of violet light back up to the wall. "Trek or saunter, patrol or wander," he read for us, speaking faster this time, as if we were supposed to catch on to something we'd missed the first time. "Underfoot you'll find me. So, whatever it is, it's...underfoot, I guess? Whether a bad day or a hard night, with the remedy I'll be rhyming. So, it's underfoot and rhymes with the remedy for a bad day. *Drink* isn't a bad guess. What rhymes with drink?"

"Stink, think, link, pink, sync, blink, wink, ink..." Piper rattled the words off, rolling her head from side to side.

"Slow down!" Bethany shouted. "I can't even think. Are any of those underfoot? Sink, maybe? Maybe it's under a claw-foot tub? Like a drain?"

"*What?*" Leo asked, brow furrowed, as confused as the rest of us.

She scoffed. "Well, I don't see anyone else offering suggestions."

"Just let me think," he said, tapping his forehead as he began to pace—back and forth, back and forth. I followed him with the beam of my flashlight just as an alert popped up on my screen.

"Shit." My heart sank.

"What?" Henry moved toward me quickly.

"What is it?" Bethany asked.

"My phone's dying."

The room fell silent, the reality of our situation finally setting in for all of us. We had no lights, no air conditioning, no electricity for all we knew, no understanding of what was going on... It was the end of the day, which meant all of our phones would soon be dying, maybe even quicker as they searched for service and maintained our only source of light.

"I have twenty-six percent left," Piper said.

"Eighteen," Leo told us.

"Twenty," Henry said.

"I have forty," said Bethany.

"I'm down to twelve," said Shane.

"Okay, so we need to conserve our batteries. Bethany, you have the most, so maybe you could be our light for a while. Everyone else should turn our lights off. Actually, maybe we'd better turn the phones off totally."

"What?" came the instant rebuttal from practically everyone in the room.

I raised my voice to speak over them. "I know it's not ideal, but we should conserve our batteries as much as we can. The longer they're on, the quicker they all die. And, once that happens, if we haven't figured a way out of here, we'll be without light completely."

I switched my phone off first, hesitating slightly as I watched the faces of my children go dark on my phone screen before disappearing altogether, then shoved it into my pocket. Eventually, everyone but Bethany did the same. With just the one light, everything felt eerier than ever. Leo pointed the black light at the wall again, reading the riddle under his breath.

"Maybe it's something to do with ink?" Bethany offered. "Like something at a desk? Something under a desk?"

He didn't look at her, shaking his head as he continued to read. "Trek or saunter, patrol or wander, underfoot you'll find me... Okay, what's under our feet?"

"The floor?" Henry answered.

"Maybe something is in the floor after all!" Bethany exclaimed.

"But floor doesn't rhyme with anything that helps with a bad day, does it? Door, more? *More*, maybe? Like...

comfort food? Maybe it's in the fridge? No, that's not under our feet... What am I missing here?" He tapped his head again, lost in thought. I stared around the room, trying to make sense of it all. What would happen if we were never able to solve this? Would we be stuck here forever? Or was this like one of those escape rooms the kids and their friends were always participating in? Would this all end after an hour regardless of what we'd been able to figure out? I wished so badly that I could text my kids, just to check in.

"Wait... Oh, wait! Wait, wait, wait!" Leo said.

"We're waiting," Henry said dryly.

When Bethany's light landed on him, his finger was in the air. "I think I've got it. It's not *drink*; that's not the remedy." He was staring into space, nodding slowly as if he was trying to convince himself.

"It's not?" Piper asked.

"No, it's *a hug*."

"A hug?" Bethany asked, sounding skeptical.

"Yes. A hug is the remedy for a bad day or hard night—"

"Aww—" Henry teased.

"Fuck off," he sneered. "*Hug* rhymes with *rug*, which is underfoot, and we trek, wander...whatever else on it." He dashed across the room. "Shine the light over here! There's a rug under the table."

Bethany followed him with the light, anticipation filling the room as we watched him pull back a corner. He ran his hands along the floorboards, searching for something loose.

"Nothing."

Could he be wrong?

He stood, moving to the next corner and threw it back.

"Here!" he shouted as Bethany rushed toward him. He held something small up in the air, examining it in the light.

"A key?" I asked, stepping forward to get a better look. It was average sized, like a door key rather than for a padlock.

"But what does it go to? How does that help us?" Henry asked.

"It's the next clue," Leo said, running a thumb over the ridges of the key.

"There's nothing else down there?" Bethany sounded disappointed. "No other riddle or anything."

"No, nothing." He pulled it up again, as if to prove the point, and Bethany moved around, shining the light as she pulled the rug back farther.

"There has to be more," Piper said. "Here, hand me the black light and let me shine it on the rest of the wall. Maybe there's another message we missed."

Leo handed it to her and she passed it over the wall slowly, looking for anything that might've slipped past us.

"Well, load of good that'll do us," Shane said.

"We should try the front door. Maybe the key will get us out of here," I suggested.

"It's worth a try." Leo stood. "We'll all go together."

With just one light now, it made it harder for us to split up for any reason, which made me feel both safer and more in danger. What if one of us was behind this?

I forced the thought away. It had been my idea to only use one light, after all.

Releasing a sigh of resignation, Piper lowered the black light, preparing to shut it off when Bethany gasped.

"Guys, wait, look..."

She pointed her light toward the rug.

"So, there was a clue under the rug, after all," Leo said, staring at the partial message the black light revealed. Bethany pulled the rug back farther to allow us to see it all, and once I'd read it, a sinking feeling filled my stomach.

The truth must come out.

CHAPTER SEVENTEEN

BETHANY

"The truth? What truth?" Henry asked, his voice filling the silent room.

"That's what all of this is about," Piper said under her breath.

"What is?" Shane asked.

"Every—"

"No," I cut her off. "It isn't."

She spoke louder then. "It has to be. Don't you see that?"

"What are you talking about?" Shane asked.

"It's nothing," I said quickly.

"Um, I would also like to know what you're talking about," Leo said with a laugh of disbelief.

"Someone knows the truth about what happened that night—" Piper started, but I cut her off.

"*Shut up!*" Stress pounded in my temples.

"What is she talking about?" Henry asked.

"They had notes on their plates," Lakynn told him. "Notes about secrets and lies."

"What?" I couldn't see his face in the darkness, but I knew he felt as sick as I did at the thought of it all.

"What kind of secrets?" Shane asked.

"It's nothing," I said quickly.

"No, I want to know what's going on," Leo said. "What kind of secrets?"

"We'll talk about this later. Right now, we just need to play the game and get out of here," I said.

"This *is* the game. Don't you see that?" Piper asked. "The truth about that night has to come out."

"That can't be what it's about." I dismissed the idea.

"What night?" Shane asked.

"Can someone please fill me in here?" Henry asked.

"My note said someone knows my secret," Piper told him. "But...since I don't have any secrets, I'm assuming it meant *our* secret."

A heavy silence sat in the dark room.

"Our secret?" Shane asked again, his tone growing worried. "What do you mean?"

"We shouldn't be talking about this," I said firmly.

"Why didn't you say anything sooner?" Leo asked.

"I've been a little preoccupied," I said, indignation filling my stomach. "And besides, that's not what mine said. Mine said someone's been lying to me. So, what's that about? Have you been lying to me, Leo?" I dug my heels into the floor. If he was going to embarrass me, two could play that game.

"What?" he asked, giving a dramatic laugh that, even in the darkness, dripped with guilt. "What are you talking about?"

"Mhm. If you want to get into it right now, let's get into it."

"Okay, guys, this is getting off topic. I think Bethany was right before; we should stick to the clues. Like the key," Henry said. "Let's check the front door like we said. If we can get out of here, we'll deal with the rest later."

"Seriously, is no one going to tell me what this is about?" Shane asked.

"Henry's right. We're getting distracted," Lakynn said firmly. "We should keep moving."

I waited for Shane to argue, but to my surprise, he remained quiet. Without another word from anyone, we headed for the hallway, making our way to the front door in tension-filled silence.

Without warning, a hand grabbed hold of my arm. I screamed, jerking out of their grasp, and flashed the light in Henry's face.

"What's wrong?" Leo asked, checking over his shoulder to see what had happened. I moved the light from his face back to Henry's.

He released me, shielding his eyes. "I scared her. Sorry. I thought she was Lakynn. Let's go." Something in his gaze caused me to falter. Lakynn stepped backward, joining us at the back of the group.

"Everything okay?" she asked.

He nodded. "Sorry." We started on our path toward the door again, but it wasn't long before I heard him say something low, practically under his breath. "I need to talk to you. Both of you."

"What?" Lakynn asked through gritted teeth.

"It's important."

"Hey, guys." I stopped moving, pretending to pant. "I'm

feeling light headed. I think it's the heat. Can one of you take a turn with the flashlight for a while?"

"'Scuse me, sorry." Leo was at my side in an instant, fanning me. "Are you okay? Do you need to sit down?"

"I'm fine. I just need to catch my breath."

"I'll stay with her," Lakynn offered quickly.

"No, I can stay," Leo said.

"No." I patted his chest. "You're the only one who's managing to figure any of this out. We need you. You should go. I'll be right behind you, I just don't want to slow anyone down because I can't keep up." I gestured toward my heels with the light.

He seemed to think for a moment before nodding. "Oh. Okay... Are you sure?"

"I'll stay back here with them," Henry said, patting Leo's shoulder. "So they aren't alone."

"Thanks," he said, holding out his hand for my phone. Once he had it, he checked in with me a final time. "Are you sure you're okay? Because I will wait with you—"

"I'm okay," I swore. "Just overheated and scared."

He kissed me gently, cupping my cheek. "I'm going to get us out of here."

"I know you are."

He turned away from me then, satisfied I was okay, and waved Piper and Shane on, light in hand. "Come on, let's go."

As they started walking, we were enveloped in darkness again.

The walls were closing in. God, it was hot. Suddenly, the fact that I couldn't catch my breath wasn't a lie.

"What's going on?" Lakynn asked.

"I think Piper's right," he whispered.

"About what?"

"About the notes. The secrets. Everything. There's something I need to tell you. And I wanted to tell the two of you before anyone else."

The group was moving quickly now, the sound of their footsteps growing fainter as they made their way down the hall and toward the front door. They had to be getting close to it.

"What are you talking about?" I asked, pushing myself away from the wall. My entire body was slick with sweat.

"I got a note, too," he blurted out. "I'm sorry I didn't tell you. I was planning to, but things were so crazy and I haven't had a chance." He was facing Lakynn from what I could tell, though it was really anyone's guess.

"A note? What did it say?" I demanded, remembering the way Henry had been pushing the last of his cake around the plate before we left. He was attempting to cover the note once he'd found it, wasn't he? Though it had probably taken him longer to notice it because he'd been talking so much.

"It said..." He paused, huffing out a breath.

"It said what?"

"It doesn't work." Leo's voice carried down the hall with a frustrated groan.

"It didn't work, guys!" Piper shouted.

"They're coming! Tell us now," I begged.

"Guys?" Piper shouted again, their voices growing closer.

Henry leaned close, lowering his voice as he gave the answer that sent chills down my spine. "It said, *I know why he died.*"

CHAPTER EIGHTEEN

PIPER

"**D**id you guys hear us?" Leo asked when we reached the spot where Bethany, Lakynn, and Henry still stood. My clothes were soaked through with sweat, sticking to every inch of me. I pulled my tunic away from my chest, fanning myself rapidly.

"Yeah." Henry gave an exhausted sigh. "Yeah, the key didn't work for the front door. Did you try both locks?"

"Mhm."

I'd never been one to say I told you so, but let's just say I was thankful for the darkness that was currently concealing my defiant expression.

"Okay, we need to try the rest of the doors, then. What about the study? And all of the doors down the other hall-way?" Lakynn said.

Without another word, we moved quickly, first checking the study door.

"No," Leo said, trying to twist the key to no avail. "Let's check the other hallway."

"Maybe someone should check the drawers in the kitchen again," Lakynn said as we neared the second hall. "We checked them earlier for a screwdriver, but have we checked them to see if there's a... I don't know, like a panic button or something? With all this security, maybe there's something to get us out."

A light illuminated the dark room and I could see her then, Bethany and Henry still standing next to her.

"Good idea," Bethany said.

"I'll go with you," Henry agreed.

The three of them were sneaking off together again, but why?

Could they somehow have something to do with this? Could they believe *we* did?

I didn't even want to be at this thing in the first place. How could they suspect me? If it wasn't for them, Shane and I would be on a date somewhere with air conditioning.

Just the thought was enough to make me sick.

I didn't want to believe it. They were my friends; they'd been my friends most of my life. I couldn't believe they could be dangerous or that they could think I would ever do anything like this, but what if I was wrong?

Someone had put us here.

Someone who knew the truth about what happened that night.

The more I thought about it, I knew I couldn't leave them alone. When they turned to walk away, I followed them.

To my surprise, they didn't protest. At first, I wasn't even sure they'd noticed me, but once they had, nothing in their demeanor seemed to change.

In the kitchen, we worked in silence, each with our phones turned back on as we searched through drawers and pulled out silverware and various kitchen utensils.

Being alone was making me paranoid.

These were my friends, including Shane, who I'd all but shut out of the night's activities, despite the fact that I was the person he was closest to here. I couldn't remember the last time I spoke to him, in fact. If it weren't for me, he wouldn't have been invited at all. He'd be somewhere safe. Cool. If anyone was angry or suspicious, it should've been him.

And, if he did get angry, if I did lose him, it would be all my fault.

I should've trusted my gut and avoided the dinner party altogether. It was what I'd wanted to do, but instead, I'd let Lakynn and Bethany convince me to come.

With that realization, I was back to worrying there'd been a reason they were so insistent. Were they trying to be sure I couldn't tell anyone what we'd done? Did they have a reason to suspect I'd already told?

"Hey, did Aaron say if he was coming home tonight? Or was he staying with Max?" Henry asked softly when Lakynn slammed yet another useless drawer closed.

"I don't know. I don't think he said," she said, frustration seeping off her rigid form. "At least, I can't remember what he said, but I assumed he was planning to stay. Why?"

He was quiet for a moment, making me freeze in place.

"What is it?" Bethany asked, and I realized we'd all stopped what we were doing.

All three beams of light hit him at once, and I watched as a wave of fear washed over his usually placid expression.

"I was just thinking... What if this isn't about us at all?"

"What do you mean?" Lakynn asked, her voice trembling. She took a half step toward him.

He looked up, meeting her eyes. "If we're all locked in here... Who's protecting the kids?"

"Hey!"

We jolted at once at the sound of someone shouting from down the hall.

Shane.

"We found something!"

CHAPTER NINETEEN

LAKYNN

I tried to ignore what Henry had said. No one was after our children. They couldn't be. I refused to believe it. Besides, there was nothing I could do from inside the house. I had to focus. Had to trust that they'd use their good sense, keep the doors locked, and call 911 if anything were to happen.

I had to believe they were safe and sound, or else I might not be able to go on. So, I forced the thoughts out of my head as we dashed down the hall toward the sound of our friends' voices, and found that the third door on the left was open, a barely noticeable blue-gray glow from outside filtering down the hall.

Henry stepped into the room first. "The key worked?"

"Yeah, just on this door," Shane said. In the dim light, I could barely see the outline of his figure walking toward us. He pointed his light in the direction of what looked like a large, pyramid-shaped stack of blocks—each block the size of our heads and the entire stack taller than any of us. Scanning the room with my phone, I realized the blocks were the only things there.

"What are we supposed to do with those?" I asked.

Henry moved toward them, nudging them gently with one foot. When they didn't move, he reached up, trying to grab one at the top. Three toppled down, and he jumped out of the way as they crashed to the ground with loud, echoing thuds.

"We should turn our phones back off," Bethany said. "Mine's dying now."

I checked the top bar of mine, the red warning taunting me. I had maybe an hour left of use, if that. Though it had been my idea initially, the thought of turning them off again, when I was just getting used to having one once more, was enough to induce fresh fear. Still, when everyone but Shane turned their flashlights off and shoved them in their pockets, I did the same.

"Shine it over here," Henry instructed, waving Shane over toward him as he reached for another block, inspecting it carefully before he tossed it to the side. Working quickly, he began to dismantle the stack. "Maybe there's something hidden underneath all of this."

I stood next to him, helping him to grab each of the blocks, checking them for any sort of clue, and tossing them next to me. Once we'd reached the bottom, with blocks scattered in every direction, I blew hair from my eyes. "Nothing. There's nothing here."

"I wonder if..." Bethany trailed off. I heard a clicking noise, then a beam of violet light illuminated the room. She gasped. "Look!"

There was something written on the back of one of the

blocks in a pile near Henry.

THINK

"Think?" I read aloud. "What does that mean? Think about what?"

"Maybe I was right before, about the drinking clue. Maybe *think* was the word that rhymed!" Shane said.

"No, I don't think so. We already solved that clue," Piper said, bending down to pick up the block. When she did, another word could be seen on a different block.

"Booze," Bethany read.

Piper laid them down next to each other, reached for another block, and turned it over in her hands.

KILLS

I swallowed.

Think.

Booze.

Kills.

I sensed the panic in the room. *Someone knows everything.*

"It's a message," Henry said softly. Piper put that block down silently and picked up the next one.

FRIENDS

"Think... Booze kills friends?" Bethany squeaked. "What are we supposed to do with this?"

"Keep looking, there might be more," Henry said.

"Yes, look!" I cried, relieved to see that wasn't all we'd been left with to figure this out. As we moved to the next pile, I immediately saw several more words in the glow of the black light. We worked our way through, turning them over carefully.

Once we'd gone through each of the piles, we stepped back, trying to get a clear picture of the scrambled message. It wasn't a perfect method—the violet beam of light only covered a few words at a time, but it was our only option, so it would have to work.

THINK

BOOZE

KILLS

FRIENDS

SOMETHING

YOUR NEXT

COVER

DISMAY

HIDDEN

SPENT

HE WANTS

A MAN

WHO

WHO

RICHES

OR TWICE

SHOES.

FASHION'S

AND
AND
AND
WHO
OF
TAKES
IN
IS
SOMETHING
TO HIS
SEARCHING
ONCE
BEEN
KNOWN
GO WITHOUT
HE'D
WILL.
HIS
LIFE
AND
CLUE
HE'D
LIES
WHAT
BENDS
TO
SAY
FOR
IS

AND HE'S
TO

She ran the light over the blocks slowly and we read each word aloud as a group as if we were on *Family Feud*, though each word only added to our confusion.

"I don't get it," Shane said eventually.

"Me either..." I trailed off.

"Is it a poem? Or another riddle?" Henry asked no one in particular.

"It's a mess, that's what it is. And it's putting us no closer to getting us home. I need to get home to see my kids. I don't have time for this. I don't want to do this," Bethany cried, the black light pointed toward the ceiling as she raised her hands.

"Just stay calm," I told her, wishing Leo would jump in to help, though he was obviously too wrapped up in solving the puzzle to try and soothe her.

"How are you so calm?" She pointed the black light at me. "How can you possibly be this calm right now? With everything that's happening?"

"I'm *not* calm, but I know we aren't going to accomplish anything by freaking out." I bit my lip, drawing in a deep breath. "We're going to get through this, okay? We are."

"How can you be sure?" Her voice cracked as she asked the question, and I felt her slam into my chest. I wrapped my arms around her, holding her tight.

Someone slipped the black light from her hands, but I couldn't be bothered to see who it was.

"Because we're going to stick together, okay? The six of

us. We can get through anything. We've proven that before, haven't we?"

She nodded, pulling away and swiping her eyes. "I just hate this. I *hate* it."

"I do, too."

"I've never liked games. I don't understand what's happening. I'm scared. And if I have to look at one more riddle, I'll—"

"That's it!" Henry said. "Hey, look! I think this is part of a sentence. We've figured part of it out."

"What?" Bethany asked, stepping back farther and turning toward the group of men. They were huddled over the blocks, one bright light and one violet light pointed down at them as they worked to place the blocks together.

"See, look. The words *your next* are on one block. I thought at first it was a grammatical error, but now I don't think so. Because if we put this here"—he slid another block next to it—"it reads *your next clue*"

"That's brilliant," I said in a breath of appreciation. "What about our next clue? Maybe the rest of the words are just here to throw us off."

"Maybe," he said, pointing at something else. "But Shane put those together. *Go without booze.* I mean, there are several combinations, but if we try to piece them together, I think we can figure it out."

"*Fashion* and *shoes* are throwing me off," Bethany said after a moment. "What do they have to do with any of it?"

"It's *fashion's*, too, with an apostrophe," I pointed out. "Fashion's what? Fashion's man? Fashion's cover?"

"We're getting ahead of ourselves," Henry said. "Let's finish one sentence at a time. Your next clue...is"—he pulled a new block over—"*hidden...* Is there an *on* or an *in* or an *under* or *inside*? Something directional?" He scanned the blocks.

"Here," Shane said, tossing one to him. "*In.*"

"Okay, excellent. Your next clue is hidden in...a man? God, I hope not." He chuckled to himself. "It's about to get real *Saw* up in here, real fast."

"In shoes?" Bethany offered, obviously still stuck on it.

"If they managed to get a clue in our shoes, color me impressed," he said, but that didn't stop him from removing both shoes and checking inside of them. Slowly, we each did the same.

"What about this one," Henry said, "*something.* Your next clue is hidden in *something.*"

Shane snorted. "Well, that's helpful."

Henry clicked his tongue. "Something what? Is there anything descriptive? Something...something... I don't know. I don't have a clue. There are too many options, but none that really fit."

"Let's look at the other sentence. Go without booze. Is there a *he*? He goes without booze? Or *she*, I guess? *They*, maybe?" I offered.

"There's...*friends.* And *he'd. He'd* go without booze. *Friends* go without booze. Either would make sense," Shane said.

"But what about the *kills* part? Are we thinking it isn't *booze kills*? Because what else would *kills* go with?" Piper asked.

"She's right. It can't be *friends kills* or *he'd kills;* booze is the only thing that makes sense," I said.

"Or *who* kills," Piper added. "Look." Her hand moved

into the beam of light, so we could see her pointing toward a few blocks near Shane. "A man who kills."

"And lies." Bethany pointed to two more. "A man who kills and lies."

"Lies and kills," I corrected. "There's a comma after kills, so I'd bet anything it comes last. *A man who lies and kills...*"

Henry snapped his fingers. "I got it. How do you like this?" He slid two more blocks in our direction. "*Think of a man who lies and kills—*"

"Well, that makes sense with the notes earlier, about secrets and lies," Piper said.

"Keep going," Bethany said, shutting down the conversation. I understood why she was doing it. Piper might trust Shane, but none of us knew him enough to trust him with our darkest secret. And, until we could talk in private without the risk of him eavesdropping, we couldn't discuss the possibility that this had anything to do with that. If we were wrong, the consequences would ruin our lives for no reason.

"Here! Here!" Shane handed him three more blocks. "*He wants* is on one block, so what if it's *who takes what he wants?*"

Bethany moved around, picking up a new block. "Ooh, not bad. What do you think, Leo? Any guesses?"

"Hey, wait!" Henry shouted, reaching out to take the block from her. "Shine the regular flashlight on this." Shane moved closer, pointing the beam at the block.

"Holy shit. Is that..."

Suddenly, there were blocks being tossed this way and that, and the black light was turned off and shoved into a pocket.

"What is it? What are you seeing?" I asked, moving closer.

"They must've been on the bottoms of the blocks when they were in the pyramid. It's why we didn't see them," Shane said.

"Here, come here," Henry said. I couldn't see whom he was talking to, but I moved in the direction of his voice.

"What is it?" I asked.

"There," Shane said. The flashlight was pointed at a stack of eight blocks.

"It's a picture," Henry explained, though now that I was on their side, I could see it, too. Or, at least, the start of it. Drawn with faint black lines, like a thin permanent marker, it was the outline of a skull.

"Turn the rest of the pieces over," Henry instructed Shane, who passed the light to me and set to work. Piece by piece, we worked together, pointing out where each piece fit into the puzzle and stacking it in place. When it was finished, we stepped back, admiring our handiwork. The skull was at least seven feet tall—so tall that it was a stretch for the men to assemble the block on the top row and just a few feet shorter than the ceiling of the room—and just as wide.

Shane patted Henry on the shoulder. "Thank God you saw that. We would've been trying to figure out the riddle all night."

"Well, let's hope this makes it easier, anyway," Henry said. Praying he was right, we moved back around the stack and someone pulled out the black light.

We gasped.

It had worked.

We'd never been meant to try to unscramble the phrase.

We'd wasted an hour trying to solve a puzzle we weren't supposed to solve.

"*Think of a man who lies and who kills...*" Henry read aloud.

At least we'd gotten that partially right.

"*Who takes what he wants and bends friends to his will. His life is spent searching for riches and booze.*" He paused. "So that's where booze fits."

"Keep reading," I urged.

"*And he's been known once or twice to...go without shoes?*"

"We would've never gotten that," Shane mumbled.

"*Your next clue is hidden in something he'd say and something he'd cover, to fashion's dismay.*"

We were quiet for a moment, letting the clues process.

"Are you sure we have the picture right?" Shane asked after a moment, moving back around to check it again.

"It's right, it's just...confusing," Henry said, with more confidence than I felt.

"Yeah, it is. Where'd they get these riddles from, anyway? They aren't very good," Shane said.

"They sound made up," I agreed.

"Okay, guys, none of this is helpful," Piper said. "Can we just think, please? I want to get out of here."

"Like the rest of us don't?" Bethany snapped.

"Leave her alone," Shane said. "We're all just tired."

"She's right, anyway," Henry agreed. "Let's think. *A man who lies and who kills...*"

"A criminal," Shane said.

Henry grumbled, as if he didn't think that was the

answer, but kept reading. "*Who takes what he wants*, so, more specifically...a thief?"

"*His life is spent searching for riches and booze?*"

"So just...any man ever?" Bethany asked dryly.

"A celebrity?" I offered. "A stockbroker?"

Henry clicked his tongue. "Maybe...but none of them really fit the whole not wearing shoes thing."

"It just says once or twice," Bethany said. "Maybe that's to throw us off. What do you think, Leo?"

"I don't know, it feels important," Piper said.

"Let's move on." Henry steered clear of the argument again. "*The clue is hidden in something he'd say and something he'd cover.*"

"How the fuck are we supposed to know what the Wolf of Wall Street would say?" Shane asked, groaning loudly.

"Or any celebrity, for that matter?" I asked. "Maybe it's a reporter? And it means that sort of *cover*, like covering a story, rather than literally covering something."

I ran a hand across my sweat-drenched neck, drying my palm on my dress. Without the electricity and air conditioning, the temperature in the house was beginning to reach beyond levels that were simply uncomfortable. How much longer could I stand this before I either passed out or was forced to start removing clothing? If I'd had any semblance of privacy, I would've torn my shapewear off hours ago.

"Guys..." Bethany said, her voice wavering slightly, pulling me from my thoughts.

"What?" I asked. Something was wrong. "What is it?"

Shane lifted the light to her, obviously sensing the concern. Her eyes were wide as she scanned the room. "Where's... Where's Leo?"

CHAPTER TWENTY

BETHANY

I clutched my stomach, gulping down breaths of air just to stay standing as Shane followed my gaze around the room with his flashlight, sweeping every corner.

"Leo?" Henry called.

"Leo?" I shouted, worry forming a knot in the pit of my stomach. "Where could he have gone?"

"When did you see him last?" Lakynn asked.

I tried to think, but my brain felt fuzzy. Jumbled. Both from the heat and the terror. "I-I don't know," I finally managed to stammer. "I mean, it's hard to keep track of everyone. I just realized I haven't heard from him since we've been in this room. Has anyone else? It's so dark I can't see anything, so I just assumed he was here, but—*Leo!*" I stamped my foot. If he was pranking me, I was going to kill him. I couldn't bear to think it could be anything worse.

"Leo? Where are you, man?" Henry asked loudly.

"He's always the first one to figure these things out, and I kept asking him for his input, but we're all talking over each other, and god, it's hot, isn't it? I'm so hot..." I fanned myself rapidly, bending over my knees. I felt as if I was going to pass out. I sank down to the ground, my breaths coming in short bursts. Suddenly, there was a hand on my bare shoulder. I squeezed my eyes shut, willing myself to breathe. To calm down. I couldn't afford to lose it right now.

I wished they'd point the light somewhere—anywhere—else.

"Come on, let's go look for him. Maybe he just got lost," Lakynn said, rubbing my shoulder gently.

"Maybe," I said, though I knew that wasn't the case. "He wouldn't have wandered off. What if something bad happened to him?"

"Let's not jump to conclusions," Henry said. I was getting mighty tired of him telling me I was overreacting to things.

With Shane leading the way, flashlight in hand, we walked out of the room and turned to our right.

"Leo?" I called, my voice trembling. "Honey, where are you? Can you hear us?"

"*Leo?*" Piper shouted.

"Leo, can you hear us? Buddy?" That was Henry, his patronizing tone unbearable.

We stopped, standing still in silence for a moment as we tried to listen. There was nothing but the pops and creaks of the old house in response.

We were moving again, stopping in the living room to check for him.

"Leo?" I called. With the curtains now pulled back in every room, there were very few options for hiding places.

Once we were satisfied he wasn't there, we checked the

dining room and kitchen, which looked just the same as we'd left them. There were no signs of a struggle. Nothing to tell us where he might've gone.

"It's like he vanished into thin air," I whispered, clutching my stomach.

Lakynn gripped my arm tighter. She might've been the only thing keeping me standing. At that point, I couldn't tell.

"We'll find him," she promised me.

"When did we see him last? Who remembers?" Henry asked.

"He was... He was with us when we tried to open the front door with the key," Piper said.

"And then when we went down the hall to check the doors," Henry said.

"We stopped," I said, recalling the instance. "We went back to the kitchen. Did he come with us?"

The room was silent for a moment, then Lakynn said, "I don't think so. It was just you, me, and Henry, right?"

"And me," Piper said.

"Oh, right. Which just leaves..."

"Me," Shane said. "He was with me when we were trying the doors. But... I don't remember if he was still with me when we actually got inside. It was so dark, and I was just excited to have found a door that opened. I thought he was with me, but maybe he went back when he noticed you guys weren't with us. It's so hard to keep track of everyone. Was he in the room when you came in, does anyone remember?"

"No," I said with a sigh. "I never talked to him, but we were just so busy, and with the darkness, you just start to assume we're all here. Did anyone else see him?" How had I forgotten to check in on my own husband? Granted, we'd nearly just gotten into a fight about his lies, and I wasn't exactly *dying* to talk to him... I paused, hating my choice of words, even if they were only in my head.

"I didn't, I'm sorry, Beth. I wasn't paying attention," Henry said from across the room. He sounded genuinely sorry. "We all have to look out for each other. We need assigned buddies to stay with, and—"

"We need to find my husband," I said through gritted teeth.

"Of course," Lakynn said. "But in the meantime, he's not wrong. We need to stick together, just in case. Check in with each other, even in the dark. Let's go back down the hall and try the doors again. Maybe he managed to get into one of the other rooms."

She didn't elaborate on why or how he would do that, or why he wouldn't have come to get us or why he wasn't responding to us shouting his name now, but I was in no state to argue. They led me down the dark hallway, lost in my own panicked thoughts as we neared the room we'd just left.

Except, when we reached the room with the open door, it wasn't the room we left.

Shane stepped back, counting the doors with the flashlight. "This isn't the same room." He reached for a closed door and twisted the handle, shoving it open. His beam landed on the stack of blocks. "*This* is the room we were in." He stepped back into the hall and pointed the flashlight at the next door, now standing wide open. "Was this room open before?"

"Leo must've gone down there," Henry said as the beam of light ran over the narrow staircase.

"Into the basement?" Lakynn asked.

I tensed, easing closer to the open door until I was standing just beside Shane. "No. He wouldn't. Why would he go down there?"

"Maybe he went back to get you all, then when he heard you coming, he accidentally went in the wrong door?" Shane offered.

"And missed the stairs?" I asked skeptically.

"Besides, the door was open when we got to the room. How would he have missed it and gone to the wrong one? There was light coming from the room you were in, from outside," Lakynn pointed out.

"Well, however it happened, we have to go look for him," Henry said. "It's the only place we haven't checked, and he may be hurt."

I couldn't bear the thought.

For a while, no one said anything. I was asking a lot of them, I knew. He was my husband. My responsibility. I wouldn't blame them if they told me I had to go into the basement alone, honestly.

I stepped forward, digging my phone from my pocket. "I'll go. You guys shouldn't have to. He's my husband."

"No way. I'm going with you," Henry said firmly.

"Me too," agreed Shane.

"Of course," Lakynn said. "We're in this together. I told you that. No one goes anywhere alone."

"Strength in numbers, right?" Piper said with a sigh.

The stairs to the basement were wooden and rickety, creaking and groaning with each step, as if warning us to turn back. I eased myself down, keeping a hand firmly on the wooden railing as we went.

"Leo?" I called, turning on my phone as I neared the bottom step. There was no way in hell I was going to be down here without a flashlight in my hand, battery be damned. "Are you down here? Are you hurt?"

It seemed everyone had the same idea I had, because as we stepped onto the concrete floor of the basement, I saw five beams of light scanning the walls. The basement was still full of stuff, boxes and exercise equipment mostly, so there were only narrow walkways to pass through.

A curtain hung on a clothesline in the middle of the room, and I squeezed my eyes shut, bracing myself before tearing it back. I whipped it across the line dramatically, then opened my eyes and exhaled.

No.

He wasn't there.

There was no sign of him anywhere.

Where are you, Leo?

I passed an open box overflowing with a taxidermied raccoon, a magic kit, and two pillows shaped like toast. It looked like some of Tom and Eleanor's stuff had ended up down there, after the move out.

Why would they have left so much?

Then again, I had more pressing issues at hand.

The basement was about twenty degrees cooler than the rest of the house, for which I was insanely grateful. Combined with the sweat on every surface of my body, the cool air was like my own personal air conditioner. I felt my senses coming back to me as I cooled down almost instantly. With a now-clear head, I walked through the space, searching desperately for any sign of my husband.

Wherever he was, I was sure he was fine.

He had to be.

I wouldn't allow myself to entertain any other possibility.

"Leo?" I called again, moving past another stack of boxes. I recognized the toe doormat that had once graced our old neighbors' front step.

Suddenly, I froze.

"Wait. Do you—"

"Hear that," I cut Lakynn off, moving toward the stairs at the sound of someone running down the hall on the floor above us. We pointed our beams of light upward, but we were too late.

The door to the basement slammed shut with a loud *THWACK*.

Click.

The click of the lock confirmed it.

We were trapped.

And we'd walked straight into it.

CHAPTER TWENTY-ONE

PIPER

"Hey, asshole!" Henry shouted, pounding a fist on the door at the top of the stairs. "Let us out of here!"

I sat near the bottom of the stairs, head in my hands as I tried to rationalize what was happening. None of it made any sense, and yet, everything made perfect sense.

It all came down to what happened that night.

I'd suspected it from the beginning, but now, it was becoming more and more obvious. I was worried something bad had happened to Leo, and that the same thing was going to happen to each of us.

Was I to blame for this?

Had I caused everything?

Crrrr...

The white noise of a speaker turning on, filled the room.

The voice was soft at first, but grew louder by the second. "How could you do this?"

I stood, white-hot lightning shooting through my body at the sound of his voice. *No.*

"Allen?"

"How could you do this?" he asked again.

Was he...crying?

"Allen, what's going o—"

"I thought I knew you," he cut me off. "But I never knew you at all, did I?"

"Allen?" Shane asked, his voice soft. "Who's Allen?" He was trying to piece it all together, and I didn't blame him, but I couldn't help him either. Nothing about this made any sense.

"What are you talking about, Allen? Hey, man, it's Henry," Henry said. His footsteps headed in my direction. "Where are you? Let's just talk about this."

"Were you ever going to tell me?" Allen demanded, and I sucked in a sharp, painful breath, realizing what was happening.

"Tell him what? What's going on?" Shane asked. "It can't be... I mean, this isn't..." He paused. "Is that *your* Allen? Your ex-husband, Allen? What is he doing here? Is he the one doing this?"

"What's going on, Piper?" Lakynn asked, her tone sharp.

"I have no idea," I said, tears stinging my eyes. "I..." But the truth was, I did know. And just like I thought, this was all my fault.

"Allen, listen—"

"You're wasting your breath," I cut Henry off.

"What are you talking about?"

"It's not him."

"Of course it is. I know his voi—"

"It's a recording." I hung my head with shame and exhaustion, feeling humiliated over the way the sound of his voice still made my heart race. "It's not him. He's not here."

"A recording? What do you mean?" Bethany demanded. She held the light in my face, as if I were a suspect in an interrogation. "A recording from what? How can you be sure?"

I batted the light out of my eyes. "It was the last fight I had with him. Before he left."

"What is he talking about? You didn't..." Her tone was rife with accusation. "You *told* him?" She gripped my arm too tight. She was angry, and I couldn't blame her. I just couldn't be made to care. Not anymore. Our secret had cost me everything.

"It's why he left me. He couldn't handle it. He said he could never look at me the same way again. Said if I could keep that secret all these years, how could he ever hope to trust me. It destroyed us... I'd never seen him look at me that way. Like I was a stranger."

"Is that why this is happening?" she demanded, and I whimpered, trying to pull my hand back.

"You're hurting me!" I cried, though no pain would ever compare to the ache in my chest over hearing his voice.

"Let her go!" Shane bellowed, his voice getting closer to us.

Bethany released my arm, more from shock than anything, I suspected.

He was standing next to me then. I could smell the woodsy scent of his cologne and I was thankful for the darkness currently concealing my guilty expression. I couldn't bear to tell him. Couldn't bear to say the words.

"Can someone please tell me what the hell is going on

here? Piper, please? What did you get me involved in? I'm trying really hard not to jump to conclusions, but—"

"Piper, you need to tell us," Lakynn said from farther away. "Is Allen the one doing this?"

"I have no idea," I said through my tears. "I swear to you, I don't. I don't know what's going on."

"It has to be him. Who else would have that recording? How do you even know it's a recording? How can you be sure? Couldn't he just be saying the same things?" Henry asked.

"I have no idea if he's the one doing it, but it's not just about the words. It's the inflection in his voice. The cracks, the pauses. I've replayed that conversation a million times. It's from the night he left. The last time I spoke to him before he filed for divorce. I'm telling you—it's a recording."

I hated myself for falling apart in front of Shane, in front of all of them, but I was too miserable to pull myself together. The wound I'd done everything to duct-tape over and glue together for the past two years had just been torn open, my insides exposed for everyone to see. How would I ever survive this again? I'd barely survived it the first time.

"I don't understand. Why would you tell him anything? It wasn't your secret to tell," Bethany said.

"I was tired of lying to him. Tired of keeping the secret. It was too big. Too exhausting. I loved him—*love* him. He was—*is*—the love of my life. But our secret was tearing us apart. I thought I could fix things if I could just be honest with him."

"But that wasn't your call to make. You should've talked to us. We all swore we'd never tell. You put every single one of us in danger, and you didn't even have the courtesy to give us a heads-up? This is your fault. If Leo is dead, it's your fault!" Bethany shouted, pointing up toward the ceiling. She was right. If something had happened to Leo, if anything happened to the rest of us, it was all my fault. My worst fear was being realized—I was going to lose them all.

Then, I really would be alone. Even more alone than I already felt.

"I never wanted to hurt any of you, but I had to tell him. It was killing me. Eating me up every single day. Every time I drove past the police station, I considered going inside and turning myself in. Every time we saw a crime happen on TV, I nearly had a panic attack. You guys wouldn't understand. You got to move on from the secret, but I never could. I still actively had to keep it every single day. I could never talk about our past. Never let anything slip that might implicate us."

"Oh, give me a break. We all lived like that. You didn't have it any worse than the rest of us," Bethany said.

"No. You don't get it. We're not the same. It was all of our secret, sure, but I was the only one having to keep it from the person I loved." I released a silent sob, reaching for the stairs and easing myself down on a step. I covered my eyes with my palms, shaking my head. "You will never understand what that was like. For twenty years, I had to lie to him every single day."

"You think we haven't had to lie to people in our lives, too?" she demanded.

"It's not—"

"Enough!" Henry shouted. "Let's not turn this into a pissing contest for who had it worse. It's done. Can we all just move on and figure out what to do to get ourselves out of here?"

I covered my face again. This was all my fault. I didn't want to argue with Bethany. I'd been selfish. I'd chosen to relieve a bit of my guilt and, in turn, I may have put them all at risk. She was right. "I'm so sorry. I don't know what his plan is, if he's even behind this. I never thought he'd leave. I thought we could get through it. I thought I could make him understand. If I'd known what would happen, I never would've told him anything. I never meant to hurt anyone."

Shane moved forward again, taking a seat next to me, and I felt his hand slide across my shoulders. I knew he didn't understand, knew he wanted answers—deserved answers—but I couldn't bring myself to say anything. I didn't deserve his support or his sympathy. It was my fault he was here.

"What did you expect to happen, exactly?" Bethany asked, looking at Lakynn and Henry to back her up, though they were both oddly silent.

Before I could answer the question, the speaker came back on, with the same white-noise sound.

Crrrr...

This time, the voice we heard was Leo. And he was crying.

"Please..." he begged. "Please."

"Leo!" Bethany shouted at the ceiling. "Oh my god, it's Leo. Leo, can you hear me? Honey, where are you?" She jumped in place, hands clutching her chest. "Are you okay?"

"Please save me," came the instant response, his words muddied by sobs.

"Leo!" Lakynn joined her cries.

"I can't do this anymore..."

"Leo, can you hear us?" Bethany shouted, practically leaping over Shane and me on her way up the stairs. She pounded on the door. "Leave him alone! Do you hear me? Leave him alone! It's not his fault, you sick bastard!"

"I hate it. I hate what we did. I hate myself... You all seem so normal. Like it doesn't affect you at all. But it affects me. It kills me." He was outright sobbing then. "I'm sorry I put you in this situation. I can't do it anymore."

"What are you talking about, honey?" Bethany asked, her tone softer. "What's going on? What did you do?"

I stood again. "Wait... *Leo's* behind this? Not Allen?"

"What's he talking about, Beth?" Lakynn asked.

She turned around at the top of the stairs, looking down at us while shaking her head. "I have no idea."

"You have to get him to let us out," Shane urged.

"Do you not think I'm trying?" She dropped her phone, slamming her fists into the door. Again. Again. Again.

Whack.

Whack.

Whack.

Whack.

When she turned back to us, she held her hands to her chest and bent down to pick up her phone. "I don't know what he's doing. What am I supposed to do?"

"Just keep talking. He'll listen to you," I said, nodding. "Talk to him. He can obviously hear us somehow. Tell him none of us are normal. Tell him we can figure this out."

The speaker was on once more. "It's too late..." came his final, whispered response. "It's too late."

CHAPTER TWENTY-TWO

LAKYNN

"Leo, please!" Bethany shouted, throwing her body against the door with all her might. "Please don't do this! It's not too late. Let us help you!"

"What's he going to do?" I asked.

"Did he call the police?" Piper asked.

"Is he going to kill us?" Shane was pacing then. "I mean, he wouldn't, right? It's not that serious, whatever you guys did, right? I mean, fine, whatever, if you're all going to refuse to tell me, I can't make you, but I wasn't even supposed to be here. I'm all Lizzie has left. I can't die in here!"

"No one's dying," I said firmly.

"Please, baby!" Bethany shouted, her face pressed to the door. "Let us out. We can talk. We'll talk. We'll turn ourselves in, if that's what you want. Just talk to us. It doesn't have to go like this. You don't want to do this."

"I just don't understand," Henry said from somewhere behind me. I searched for him with my flashlight.

"Don't understand what?" I asked. Above us, Bethany stopped banging on the door long enough to listen.

"If Leo's really the one behind this, how did he manage to pull it off? I mean, I'm sorry, Beth, but he's not exactly a rocket scientist. He likes games, sure, but all of this? How? He was conspiring with Penn and Etta somehow? How would he even know them? He works from home, it's not like they're his coworkers none of us have met. And we know all of his friends. Are they police? Did he hire them? I mean, come on, they could still be messing with us."

"And what? Forcing him to say everything he just said?" Bethany asked.

"Exactly. For all we know, they *are* forcing him to say it."

"Well, that's almost worse, Hen," she said with a sob. "Because that means they have him and they're hurting him, or maybe worse."

"But it also means he's still alive, and not trying to hurt us. There's still time for us to save him," he said. "We just have to get out of the basement and figure out how to get to him."

"And how would you suggest we do that, Henry? She's going to dislocate her shoulder if she keeps banging into the door like that. It's obviously not budging," Piper said.

"The door is solid and the walls are concrete. We aren't going to be able to break out, so we need another way."

"Like what?" I asked. I recognized the hope in his voice and suspected he had a plan.

He kept his voice low as he spoke. "There was a dinner with Tom and Eleanor once—I think the one where he hired the magician, but maybe it was the couple's game show night

—anyway, he mentioned that when he had the place built, he had them build tunnels underneath it. Hidden passages with access to every room. The works, as he called it."

"You're right! I remember that, too," Bethany said, moving down the stairs hesitantly, as if it physically pained her to leave the basement door, each foot dangling over the steps for several seconds before landing.

"If we can figure out how to access the tunnels, maybe we can find a way out of here," he said simply.

"But how? Tom didn't show us where they were. For all we know, he was just kidding, anyway," I argued. "Even if they're real, what are we supposed to do? Pull books off shelves? Knock on the walls until we find a hollow one? It's impossible. Besides, as long as we're down here, we can't do anything."

"But what if we could find some sort of map? I mean, this looks like the rest of Tom and Eleanor's stuff. If a map exists, this is where it would be." He shrugged.

"He's right. A lot of their stuff is still down here," Bethany said.

"It's worth a shot at least," Henry urged. "We don't have any other plans."

I was skeptical, but still, I said, "Okay." I moved to the nearest box. "Are we just looking for something labeled *map?* Or is this going to be hidden on the back of the Declaration of Independence or something?"

"I don't think he'd label it so blatantly," Henry said, not appreciating my humor. "But if you see any papers, just look through them. It might look more like blueprints than a treasure map."

"Are you going to help?" Bethany asked. I scanned the room, trying to see whom she was addressing. Everyone was up, already searching through boxes.

Except Shane.

He was standing in the middle of the basement, several feet from us, eyes darting back and forth in thought as he scraped his bottom lip with his teeth.

"Shane?" Piper called.

"Something you just said gave me a thought," he said, wagging a finger in our general direction.

"What?"

"A treasure map..."

"Yeah, what about it?" Henry asked, already tearing through the box nearest him.

Shane snapped his fingers. "Guys, I...I think I just solved the riddle."

"What are you talking about?" Bethany asked. "We've moved on from that."

"I know, I just... I don't know, when we get up there, it might make sense to have some direction," he said softly. "I want to get out of here, and if solving these riddles is the way, then I'm all for it."

"Fair enough," Henry said.

"Unless the riddles are a way to waste our time. Leo's counting on us," Bethany said.

"I want to hear him out. He's right. We need a plan. Right now, these riddles are all we have to go on." He paused, waiting for Bethany to argue, but she didn't. "So, what did you figure out?" He dropped a box to the ground, waiting.

"I think the answer is..." Shane hesitated, not immediately meeting our eyes in the bright glares from our flashlights. "Could it be *pirate?*"

"Pirate?" Piper asked.

"Yeah, the treasure map thing made me think about it—"

"What were the clues again?" I asked, racking my brain for them.

"I don't remember them all, but there was the line about searching for riches and booze. And going without shoes. That could be a pirate, right?"

"And he lies and kills," Piper said softly. "Bends friends to his will. Do pirates have friends?"

"They have a crew..." Shane shook his head. "Maybe I'm wrong."

"No, I think you could be onto something," Henry said. "It all fits. That would explain the skull picture, too. Good work, Shane."

"Well, I don't see any pirates down here, do you?" Bethany asked, hands out to her sides.

"I wouldn't put it past Tom to have owned a few statues or something. Or a buried treasure, for that matter. So, maybe a treasure map is what we're looking for after all."

"No, wait," I said, thinking back. "The next clue is hidden in...something he'd say, right?"

"What do pirates say?" Piper asked.

"Arrg?" Shane offered.

"What was the last part?" Henry asked.

"Something he'd cover, to fashion's dismay," Bethany recited.

"Something he'd say and something he'd..." I froze. "*Eye.* The answer is eye. It has to be."

"As in 'aye, aye, Captain?'" Shane said.

"And an eye patch," I agreed, covering my own eye as I said it.

"So something's hidden in our eyes?" Piper whined, a hand moving instinctively to her cheek.

"Holy shit," Henry whispered, "I was joking earlier about the *Saw* twist. They can't really expect us to..."

"I'm not going to do anything with my eye. You can forget it," Bethany said firmly, taking a step back from us.

"Even if it means Leo's life?" Henry asked. Though I knew he sounded confident to everyone else, I heard the fear in his voice. He was trying to act tough, but he was scared. We all were.

"Wait." I froze.

Thinking.

Thinking.

"I just remembered something."

"What?" Henry asked.

"I don't think the answer is our eyes. How would that even be possible? This isn't a horror movie. I think it's hidden in an eye in the house."

Sounding relieved, Bethany said, "I saw a taxidermied raccoon earlier. Do you think it could be there? Or in one of Eleanor's creepy dolls?"

"I was actually thinking of something bigger."

"Bigger?" Henry asked.

"Do you all remember the two windows down here?" I spun around, searching for them.

They were quiet for a moment, but then I heard Henry ask, "The eye-shaped windows? Oh my god, why didn't I think of that? Tom was so proud of them. He said they looked like the house had its face buried underground and had come up for a peek around." He spun around, rushing forward. "There's one over here, I think!" He hurried past me, stopping briefly to kiss my forehead. "That was brilliant."

The windows were hidden behind stacks of boxes, and it was so dark outside they weren't providing any light, but once we'd cleared the space in front of them, the beams of our flashlights reflected off the glass a few feet above our heads.

"These won't open either, and even if we could break through them, they're too small to climb out of," Henry said, running his fingers across the ledge. *"But..."* His grin broadened.

"Did you find something?" Piper asked.

He pulled his hand down, a fistful of items tucked between two fingers and a thumb. He dropped them into his other hand so we could examine them.

A key and two notes.

He turned the first one over, so the word **Confess** was on full display. He looked up, only briefly, as if surveying our reactions, then turned the second note over. This one simply said: **8:00**.

"So, we're supposed to confess at eight?" I asked, checking the watch on my wrist. "It's nearly ten. We missed the deadline."

"Maybe that's why they took Leo," Henry said.

"*If* they took him," Piper murmured.

"We're running behind," Henry snapped. "We've spent

too much time scrambling and arguing. Let's just focus, please."

I couldn't help thinking of the time we'd wasted on the blocks, trying to unscramble the impossible riddle.

If we hadn't wasted so much time, would Leo still be with us?

"They wanted us in the basement," Bethany said. "After we solved the riddle, they wanted us in the basement to find the key." She pointed the beam of light toward the top of the stairs. "Maybe now that we have it, they'll let us out."

"Let's see," Henry said.

Together, we eased our way toward the top of the stairs, Henry in the lead and me close behind him. I could hear Bethany's ragged breathing just behind me, her hand on my back as Henry lifted the key toward the lock on the door. In an instant, he froze.

"What's wrong?" I asked.

"The lock is on the other side," he said, shining his light to prove the point. "There's nowhere for me to even put the key."

"Wait, seriously?" I ran my hand along the plate under the doorknob in disbelief. How was this possible? "So, what now?"

"I don't—"

Not waiting for his response, Bethany shoved past us. "Let us out of here!" she bellowed, her screams panicked and beastly.

She grabbed the doorknob, twisting it with all her might, and gasped.

To our surprise, we heard a click.

The door opened a half inch.

She jerked her hand back, as if the knob had scalded her.

"What the..." Henry pushed the door open farther.

Then, we heard the scream.

CHAPTER TWENTY-THREE

BETHANY

We raced down the hall, toward the sound of the screams. As we did, I tried to decide if they sounded like Leo. Tried to decide how to brace myself for what I was walking into. But I couldn't tell. It didn't sound exactly like him, but I had no idea what he'd been through. What if they were torturing him? What if they were killing him?

We stopped too soon, and I slammed into something. Henry groaned loudly.

"Sorry."

"Easy. You okay?" he asked, turning to face me.

The wind had been knocked out of me, but I couldn't focus on that. "Where's it coming from?"

"One of these two doors," he said. He shoved his phone back into his pocket. "Shane, get in front. Lakynn, Piper, keep Bethany back. Keep the lights on us."

"Like hell," I argued. "I'm coming, too."

"Just let us see what we're getting into," Henry said,

lifting the key to the door as Shane shoved his phone into his own pocket. As Lakynn held hers out, I spied the one percent warning that popped up on the screen. We had just minutes of battery left with hers. I lifted mine, which wasn't doing much better with under ten percent already.

Henry turned the key in the lock.

Click.

I squeezed my eyes shut, preparing for the worst, as I felt the gush of air hit my face.

"Give me the light," Henry said, taking Lakynn's phone from her. Shane slid my phone from my hands without asking for permission. I was too weak to argue. Both of Lakynn's arms went around me.

He's dead.

This is it.

He's dead.

But if he's dead, how is he still screaming?

I opened my eyes, taking in what I was able to see. There was no body. No blood. No Leo.

In fact, the room seemed empty except for the blaring sound of the screams, but it wasn't the room itself—the walls, the floor, the ceiling—that the flashlight beams were focused on. Instead, they were directed at the clock on the wall. A giant grandfather clock with a cheerful clown face.

It was screaming at us.

Suddenly, I realized it was the same scream we'd heard when we first arrived at the house.

This was the clock the Harringtons had told us about.

"Make it stop," Lakynn said, covering her ears.

I stood still, mesmerized by it.

Leo's not dead.

There's still a chance.

"I thought he said they turned this off," Shane said, examining the side.

Henry reached up, opening the glass face and urging the hands forward. Once they were off of the ten, the screaming ceased.

We breathed a collective sigh of relief.

"Guys, look," Lakynn said, drawing our attention back to her. "What's all over the walls?"

Blood.

Leo's blood.

He's dead.

We're too late.

I dropped to my knees without warning, too weak to stand, but still, I couldn't peel my eyes away from the sight as Shane and Henry moved the lights to the wall, giving us a clear view of what she was pointing at.

The feeling in my hands came back.

It wasn't blood, but rather scraps of paper.

Newspaper.

Upon further inspection, I realized we were staring at the same newspaper clipping over and over again. There were over one hundred of them, all pinned to the wall in a random pattern. As if whoever had done it was doing so in a manic state. I pushed myself up from the floor, dusting off my hands as I tried to catch my breath.

"What the hell..." Henry tore one from the wall.

I didn't need to move any closer to know they were about Tyler Kingston.

I recognized his picture immediately.

Dark hair.

Dark eyes.

Too skinny.

"Who is this?" Shane asked, pulling a second clipping down and reading it. "Some missing kid from...twenty-five years ago?" His brows shot up. "Hold on, is this what you all were talking about in the basement?" His face was marked in shadows, but I sensed he was scanning each of our expressions for guilt. "Did you all have something to do with this?" He released a nervous laugh, as if he thought it was ridiculous, then swallowed, taking a step back. "Did you?"

"Look, it's complicated..." Lakynn said, but it was clear Shane wasn't listening. Instead, his light was scanning the room.

"Wait." He dropped the paper, his face filled with panic. "Where's... Where's Piper?"

CHAPTER TWENTY-FOUR

LAKYNN

S weat dripped from every inch of my skin as we raced around the room, searching for Piper.

"Piper, where'd you go?" Shane called.

"Piper!" I couldn't breathe. Couldn't focus. No longer caring what I looked like or what anyone thought, I stopped briefly, hiking my dress up and reaching for the top of my shapewear. I peeled it from my skin inch by inch, receiving instant relief at the feeling of fresh air. I tossed the material down, resuming the search.

"Shit," Henry murmured.

I turned to face him, though I couldn't find him in the dark. My stomach plummeted.

"Henry?"

"I'm here. Your phone died."

Relief was quickly replaced by new worry. Our phones were all dying. What little battery they'd had when we arrived was quickly being drained by our flashlights. But what choice did we have? What other options were there?

"Piper!" I shouted, cupping my hands around my mouth and praying she could hear me and would answer.

"She was in the back of the line up the basement stairs. Do we know she made it back up here?" Henry asked.

"She was right beside me," Shane said. "But then we heard the screams and...I-I-I don't know. I don't know when we lost her."

"People seem to go missing around you a lot," Bethany pointed out.

"What's that supposed to mean?" he demanded.

"It's just suspicious, that's all."

"What's suspicious? I care about Piper. I would never do anything to hurt her, you know that!" he shouted.

"I'm just saying—"

"Knock it off, both of you," Henry yelled. "I'm tired of listening to it. We're all exhausted, hot, and scared, but this isn't helping anything. Bethany, all you've done is pick fights with everyone all night. Just drop it, okay? Shane was with us. He didn't have time to hurt Piper without us noticing. Whoever's doing this, this is what they want. They want us fighting and going against each other, okay?"

"Well, excuse me if I'm emotional, Henry. My husband is missing, probably dead, but let me just suck it up and put a smile on my face for you," she sneered.

"What if Piper was right all along? What if we were supposed to confess? What if that's the only way to get out of here?" I asked, trying to head off the fight. "That's what the note said, after all. *Confess.*"

"It said confess at eight. We missed it," Bethany said.

"What if it meant eight in the morning?" Shane suggested.

"We're going to be stuck here all night?" she whined.

"Wait, no. It didn't say confess at eight," I said, shaking my head.

"Yes, it did, remember?" Henry moved toward me, holding out his hand in the light beam and revealing the notes once more.

I picked them up, examining them. "There's nothing that says 'at' here, though. The eight is separate."

"What do you mean?" Bethany asked.

"Earlier, you said they wanted us in the basement." I pointed in the direction of her voice. "When we found the clue that was supposed to take us to the basement, the door magically opened." I was thinking out loud at that point. "And...and then once we had the key, the key to unlock this room, when we needed to be up here, the basement door was suddenly unlocked, even though we'd all been trying to beat it down for an hour or more."

"What are you saying?" Shane asked.

"I'm saying...this is all orchestrated. They're sending us where they want us. We heard the screaming to let us know what room to go in. That can't be a coincidence." I glanced at the clock. "So, if our next clue is eight, we should be looking for an eight." I walked forward, pulling back the glass over the clown face with trembling, cautious hands as if I expected it to lean forward and bite me.

I jerked my arms back as someone stepped behind me, but the tension melted away as I recognized the sounds of Henry's breathing. I wasn't doing this alone.

We were all together.

Lifting up on my tiptoes, I ran a finger across the number eight on the clock face.

A smile played on my lips. "I was right. There's a button here. The number eight is a button."

I glanced over my shoulder, where Henry was waiting. He put a hand on my waist. "Push it."

I sucked in a deep breath, closing my eyes and counting to three in my head. With a sharp exhale, I pushed the button and prayed for a miracle.

Then, the lights came on.

CHAPTER TWENTY-FIVE

BETHANY

I shut one eye, trying to adjust to the blinding lights overhead. At first glance, the group looked as if we had just survived a natural disaster or action movie. Our clothing was rumpled and dirty, the material drenched in sweat.

Lakynn's usually sleek hair had frizzed in every direction, curls gathering at the nape of her neck. Loose tendrils of hair hung down from my braid, frizzing too.

Our makeup had all sweated off in streaks and blotches; she had dark circles of mascara under her eyes that I imagined matched my own. Henry had taken off his suit jacket at some point, and Shane's shirt was unbuttoned over halfway down.

I searched their faces, hoping desperately to lay eyes on a disheveled version of my husband, but to no avail. My heart sank.

"The lights are back on," Lakynn said, glancing around the mostly empty room. I couldn't tell whether she sounded happy. "Does that mean it's over?"

"Maybe." Henry didn't sound convinced. "Come on, stay close." He led the way across the room, peered left, then right, out into the hall, and waved us forward. "Leo? Piper? You guys out here?"

We made our way down the hall and turned right, headed for the front door.

"Wait, we can't—"

"We can't leave them," Shane said, interrupting me when I tried to say something similar.

"I just want to see something," Henry said without looking back. We reached the front door within a few moments, and I held my breath as he outstretched his hand toward the doorknob.

Nothing happened.

"It's still locked?" I asked, my chest deflating with slashed hope.

Henry nodded, his lips pressed into a thin line when he turned to face us. "I don't think it's over yet."

"But there were no more clues," Lakynn said. "The button just turned on the lights, it didn't give us another clue."

"Right, but we still have one clue we didn't follow." He nodded, retreating back down the hall on high alert, his eyes darting this way and that, body stance low and wide, hands out as if ready to attack.

I spun on my heel to follow him. "Which one?" I asked.

When we reached the second hallway, he turned back to us, holding out the crumpled, sweaty notes in his palm. The ink had begun to bleed from moisture, but the message was still clear:

Confess

"I think, until we've all confessed, that people are going to keep going missing." His jaw was tight as he spoke.

"What do you mean?" I asked, dread washing over me. Hadn't we all but confessed here tonight? These creeps knew about Tyler. What more did they want?

"Leo and Piper both disappeared when they told a lie," he said, the words sucking air from my lungs.

"What?"

"What are you talking about?" Shane demanded. "What lie?"

Henry's calm demeanor remained unwavering. He fixed his gaze on the wall as he spoke. "You asked Leo if he was lying to you, because of your note at dinner, but he said no. That was a lie, and minutes later, he was missing—"

"How do you know—"

"Piper told us all that she was the one who told Allen the truth. That was also a lie, and now she's missing, too. I don't think those are coincidences."

I cocked my head to the side, trying to make sense of what he was saying.

Lakynn was the first to respond. "And you know all of this for a fact? How do you know they were lying?"

Henry closed his eyes, his shoulders slumping. "Because Leo is the one who told Allen the truth about what we did that night. He told me about it after. They were drinking, and it slipped out. Allen confronted Piper, and she confessed." His expression was blank when he looked up to meet my eyes, then Lakynn's. "Allen couldn't handle it."

Why hadn't Leo told me about that?

Why had he never mentioned telling Allen what we did?

Did he think I'd be angry? He'd be right.

But I thought we told each other everything.

Almost everything.

I released a puff of air through my lips. "So *that's* what Leo was lying about, then? That he told Allen the truth?"

Henry was slow to nod. "That *and*..." He paused. "I'm sorry, Beth. It's the only way to get us out of this."

"Go ahead." Ice took hold of my organs as I braced myself for his next words.

"He was using again."

I released my breath, staring at him. Waiting for him to say more.

"What?" It was Lakynn who gasped in horror. Lakynn, with her perfect life and perfect husband.

"I don't know when it started, but he came to me a few months ago asking for some pain pills. Said he'd pulled a muscle in his back. I told him he needed a prescription, but... you know how he gets. He acted like I was being ridiculous, like we didn't go back so far. So, I gave him a few." Finally, regret had made its way through to Henry's cold expression. "Just enough to last him the weekend. I told him if he needed more, he'd have to go to the doctor."

"And that was it?" I asked, but I already knew the answer. I'd known it the day I found a bottle of pills under the mattress six months ago.

"No. There were a few other times, here and there. But finally, I cut him off. And, once I had, he started stealing from me. I caught him twice, but I assume it happened more than that. I threatened to turn him in if he didn't get help, or to tell you, but by that point, he was so far gone..."

He looked away, his voice losing power. "He threatened to turn me in, too. I could've lost my license. My business.

Piper overheard us arguing one day last week. After I caught him trying to steal while I was trying to help a customer. Leo was the angry customer she was asking about at dinner. We both convinced her it was no big deal, that I could handle it, but she was always suspicious. She wouldn't let it go." He swiped his eye with a fist. "He couldn't handle it. We all knew he was the weakest link, even back then. It ate at him. Destroyed him. What happened that night sobered the rest of us, but it drove Leo to drinking and using even more." He paused, drawing in a long inhale, and for a moment, I thought he was done. "What you heard in the basement, what he was saying, he wasn't talking to you. He was talking to me."

"How could you possibly know that?" I asked.

"Because it already happened. Like Allen's voice, Leo's was a recording, too. He was apologizing to me after Piper saw us. Telling me he was sorry he put me in that situation. Telling me he couldn't handle it. Saying it was too late. He was too far gone. He needed help, but I was too worried about saving my own ass to get it for him. I'm so sorry, Beth." His posture crumbled, his expression heavy and regretful. "I never thought..."

I took a step back from him as he reached for me, feeling disgusted. Both with him and myself.

Before I could say anything, I heard another noise from down the hall and directed my attention toward it.

Creeeaaaaak...

To our left, another door in the hallway eased open slowly, just as the basement door had done.

Henry's eyes widened and he nodded. "I was right. It's working. We have to confess."

He took a few steps toward the door and pushed it open. Once inside, he gasped.

I darted toward him, no regard for my own safety as I feared the worst. I stopped in the doorway as if I'd run into a sheet of glass. My knees grew weak.

"Oh my god," Lakynn whispered breathlessly from just behind me.

In front of us, there was a message. One that looked as if it had been fingerpainted on the wall with sticky, red blood.

The truth shall set you free.

CHAPTER TWENTY-SIX

LAKYNN

W e checked behind the door before crossing the room, just in case, then turned our attention back to the ominous message. Underneath it, there were three envelopes taped to the wall in a neat row.

As we got closer, I could see that the envelopes were each labeled.

Lakynn
Henry
Bethany

I slowly reached for the envelope with my name on it, the tape peeling a bit of the paint from the wall, revealing the lavender color the room had once been painted.

"Should we open them?" Bethany asked, holding hers delicately in her hands, as if it were a bomb waiting to detonate.

I nodded, swiping a fingernail under the edge of the envelope and tearing it open. Inside was a single sheet of paper with a scrawled note on it.

Tell him about that night.

My eyes flicked to Shane, my pulse erratic. "Why don't you have one?"

"I have no idea," he said, running a hand over the wall where the letters had been. "Why don't Piper or Leo? This had to all be prepared beforehand, didn't it?"

"If so, they must've known they'd be taking them," I said. "Which throws out Henry's theory about the lies."

"They could've put all of these in here when we were in the basement," Bethany said.

"Then why doesn't Shane have one?" I demanded, pointing a finger at him. Suddenly, Bethany's theories didn't seem so far fetched. He *had* been the one with Leo and Piper when they disappeared, hadn't he? And he was the newest member of the group.

What if he was behind it?

What if he'd been coordinating it from the get-go?

But what did he have to gain?

"He wasn't supposed to be here. He isn't part of this," Henry said, putting a hand on my shoulder. "This is about what we did that night. We have to confess." He gave a resigned nod.

I pressed my envelope to my chest. "I don't want to do this."

"I know." He squeezed my shoulder, rubbing a thumb

over my collarbone. "I know. But it's the only way to get out of here and protect our kids. If Shane decides to tell—"

"I'm not going to tell anyone anything," Shane said. "Just please, for the love of God, if you know what the hell is happening, please get us out of it."

"If *whoever's* doing this decides to tell," Henry corrected himself, "then it is what it is. But I can't put anyone at risk to save myself again. I just can't. We aren't those people anymore." His gaze lingered on mine, and he let his hand leave my shoulder before he turned to meet Bethany's eyes.

"We have to save Leo," she said, her voice trembling. "And Piper. They're counting on us."

Henry nodded solemnly. "What does your note say?"

She turned it around slowly. "*How do you live with yourself?*" She squeezed her eyes shut, and a fat tear trailed down her cheek. "And the truth is, I have no idea." More tears spilled out of her eyes then. "I knew about Leo's drug problem, but I hadn't gotten the nerve to confront him. I didn't want to talk about that night. I didn't want to relive it. The truth is, we all have our own coping mechanisms—your humor, Henry, Leo with the drugs, Lakynn's perfectionism, the fact that I work myself to death—we're all managing the best way we know how, but we're surviving. None of us are living. Not really. I regret that night every single day of my life. I wish I could go back and fix it, I do. It haunts me just like it does all of you, just like Leo. And now, maybe I'll never get the chance to tell him that—"

The lights flipped off again, bathing us in darkness.

"I'm telling the truth!" she screamed. "I'm doing everything you've asked."

A faint humming sound filled the room, and a black light

flickered overhead. Shane's shoes, Henry's shirt, and our four smiles were all that could be seen—faceless teeth floating in the room.

"Look!" Shane said, his smile disappearing. I searched for my phone before remembering Henry still had it and it was dead, anyway.

I turned to see what he was telling us to look at and gasped at a black-light message on the far wall.

Lake Alton, Slip 238

"What does that mean?" I asked. "Are we supposed to go there? We can't get out of here!"

"No. It's a message for me," Bethany said, and the lights flicked back on. A confirmation.

I shot a glance at the ceiling, trying to understand how any of this was happening. How were they controlling the lights and doors? How were they watching and hearing us?

"What do you mean it's a message for you?" Shane asked.

"I'm not confessing the right secret," she said. When I looked her way, she wouldn't meet my eyes.

"What does that mean?" I repeated Shane's question.

She looked at Henry then. "What does yours say?"

He turned it around and read it aloud. *"Tell her the truth about that night."*

"Her?" I asked. "Her who? Mine says tell him what you did that night. I assumed it meant Shane."

They exchanged a look and Henry nodded at her. "It should be me," he said simply.

Suddenly, it felt like the room was spinning around me.

No.

No.

No.

I knew what was coming. I could sense it in the way they were looking at me. In the guilty looks on both their faces.

"We need to tell you something," Henry said, then corrected himself. "*I* need to tell you something. It's about that night."

CHAPTER TWENTY-SEVEN

BETHANY

Twenty-Five Years Ago

The leaves crunched underfoot as we moved through the long stretch of woods outside of town. I was late and it was getting dark, but it didn't matter. I could've made my way down the overgrown, unmarked path with my eyes closed; we'd walked it so many times.

"Whoo! Sexy lady! Would you like some fries with that shake?" Someone slapped my butt from behind, then covered my eyes, purring in my ear. The warm, vanilla scent of her perfume hit my nose.

I rolled my eyes, pulling away. "Very funny, Lake."

"Aww, you're no fun," she teased, snatching the bottle of wine from my grasp and twisting off the cap to take a swig.

I snatched it away from her. "Slow down. That's for everyone."

"Ow," she whined, rubbing her finger over her lip. "I think you busted my lip." When she pulled her hand away, I could see the pink tinge of blood over her front teeth, but she laughed anyway and dashed ahead, flipping her hair over her shoulder. "Keep up, slowpoke."

She was already drunk; I could tell by the carefree way she moved—half-run, half-skip—legs flying behind her as she went. Since her parents' separation, Lakynn had been spiraling, which meant she had access to more liquor than usual, and our parties had gotten more frequent and much wilder.

When we reached the usual gathering place, Henry and Leo were already there, sitting next to the fire in the center of the clearing.

Lakynn rushed toward Henry, placing a sloppy kiss on his neck from behind.

"Hey, good-lookin'," he said, pulling her around so she lay in his lap. He kissed her lips. "Missed you."

"Missed you more." She rubbed her nose over his.

Barf.

I rolled my eyes, again, cringing inwardly as I made a point to find a large rock far away from them and sit down. The smoke from the fire burned my lungs, but I wouldn't dare move closer. They'd just gotten back together, so there was no doubt they were going to be annoyingly sweet and grossly inappropriate all night.

"Hey, Bethany," Leo called from across the fire. He lifted a stick in the air, waving it at me.

I waved a finger at him, not really paying attention. "Hey."

Within a few minutes, Lakynn had repositioned herself on Henry's lap, her legs on either side of him. I could hear the sounds of their make-out session from several feet away. "So," I said loudly, hoping to interrupt.

"I brought wine from my aunt's stash. What have the rest of you got?"

Leo reached under his chair, revealing a pack of juice boxes and a half-empty bottle of vodka. "Nice," Henry said, swatting his arm. "I have the usual." He kicked a box of beer at his feet.

"And I—" Lakynn climbed off Henry's lap finally, brushing her long, dark hair from her eyes as she reached into her bra and pulled out two large handfuls of tiny, plastic bottles of alcohol. "Brought a buffet."

"Jackpot," Henry cried as he tossed a few to Leo and a few to me.

"Save some for me," came a voice from the edge of the woods.

"Hey, hey! Now it's a party. Gang's all here," Leo said, standing up and outstretching a hand as the two figures came into sight. Piper dropped a bottle of whiskey in front of my feet, sitting down on the rock next to me.

"Hey." She grinned. She smelled of weed and beer, and I suspected they'd started the party without us on the way over.

"I thought you were grounded," I said, furrowing my brow at her.

"I am. I'm home in bed right now." She winked, leaning over to kiss the boy who'd just sat down next to her.

"Hey, Tyler," I said, picking up the bottle of whiskey in front of me and taking a drink. I winced as it burned my throat. "What'd you bring?"

He reached into his side pocket, pulling out a bag of white powder and two joints. He grinned wickedly as he waved them in the air. "You know I hooked us up."

The group howled with delight, as if we were a pack of wolves, and that night, we might as well have been.

Wild, carefree, untamed...

There were no rules in the woods.

No parents.

No teachers.

No homework.

No jobs.

Just us.

In the woods, it felt like nothing else mattered or existed at all.

———

At some point, Leo ended up next to me on the rocks, but by that time, I was so completely trashed I didn't mind when he tried to kiss me. In fact, some part of me liked it.

"Oooh," Lakynn teased, her voice in my ear. I hadn't even realized she was there.

I swatted her away.

"Kissy, kissy, kissy..." She was back in my ear, cackling loudly, and I heard Leo laughing.

She ran her tongue over my cheek and Leo let out a loud, "*Whoop!*"

She giggled, leaning away, obviously enjoying the attention.

"She's fucking toasted," Henry said from farther away, his words slurring.

"So are you," she said, standing up and toppling backward. I reached out a hand to stop her, but it was no use. She fell to the ground with a loud thud, inches from the fire. On impact, she released loud, boisterous laughter, curling into a ball and rolling onto her side.

"Whoa. Easy does it," I heard Henry saying. He stood, reaching for her. "I'm not trying to let you die in a fire tonight, okay? What do you say we sit down over here where it's safe?"

"No! You're my seat!" she screamed drunkenly, cackling as he pulled her to her feet.

"Yeah? Well, come prove it." He was kissing her again, guiding her back to the rock he'd been sitting on earlier, and I forced myself to look away, the liquor souring in my stomach.

"Hey, guys, where's Tyler?" Leo asked.

The question sobered me a bit. I searched around for him, trying to stand.

"He needed a pee break," Piper said, reaching for another beer. "Or so he said. Really, I think he's hogging all the *blow for himself,*" she shouted the last few words, taking another swig of her whiskey.

"Hey, Piper, if you're worried about it, I've got some blow for ya," Henry said, grabbing the crotch of his pants, his tongue hanging out with silent laughter.

"In your fucking dreams," she groaned, flipping him off.

Next to me, Leo's face was red from laughter.

"Miss me?" Tyler asked, running out of the woods without his shirt on. He leaped up, standing on top of a rock, and threw a tiny bottle of vodka into the fire.

The fire exploded and everyone cheered. My face was so hot, but I couldn't summon the urge to move.

"Get over here," Piper told Tyler, wagging a finger at him.

"With pleasure." He jumped down, running toward us at full speed and skidding across the dirt.

"Put your shirt on," she said, rolling her eyes and reaching across him.

"Since when do you want me to put my clothes back *on?*" he asked slyly, but slid it over his head anyway before kissing her.

"You okay, Beth?" Henry asked. I nodded, though my head was too heavy to tell. Leo's hand was on my leg, but I couldn't remember when he put it there.

I hung my head, closing my eyes for just a second, and trying to get my bearings. When I looked up, I had no idea how much time had passed. I'd spilled the drink in my hand, the warm beer puddling around my tennis shoes.

On the other side of the fire, Lakynn had stripped down to her bra and mismatched boy-short underwear, and was dancing around aimlessly. The three boys were gathered together, watching with obvious fascination.

At one point, Henry pulled out a wad of cash and tossed it at her. Most of it landed in the fire, but no one seemed to notice. Tyler stood up, dancing next to her. He whispered something in her ear.

I could still hear her laughter as I fell back on the ground behind me, staring up at the stars. When I looked over, I realized Piper lay there, too. She grinned at me, her face hazy, and I grinned back.

This—this feeling of fading into oblivion—was all I really wanted. Just one fucking night a week when we could shut everything else out and not feel a single thing.

Piper locked her pinkie with mine and I closed my eyes, the comfort of sleep pulling me in. I welcomed it.

SCREAMS TORE ME FROM SLEEP.

"Guys! Something's wrong! Guys! Seriously!"

"Stop!"

"Get back!"

"What the fuck?"

A mashup of voices filled the air, all muddled together and panicked. I couldn't tell who was speaking as I sat up, rubbing my eyes and trying to figure out where I was. I pulled leaves from my hair, one eye squeezed shut as I tried to make sense of what I was seeing.

"What's wrong?" I croaked.

The group was huddled in one spot to the left of the fire, behind the rock circle. Lakynn turned and spotted me first. She leaped over the rocks, rushing to my side and tugging me to my feet. She was dressed again, although her shirt appeared to be on backward. "Come on, wake up, we need your help. Something's wrong with Tyler."

I stumbled, trying to wake myself from sleep as I made my way toward the rest of the group.

"This is really bad, guys," Piper said. I realized she was crying when I saw what they were looking at. "What do we do?"

Tyler was lying on his back on the forest floor, his eyes wide but unresponsive. When I got closer, I saw a trail of vomit spilling out of his mouth.

Henry had crouched down next to him. He shook Tyler, the gravity of the situation evident on his face. "Tyler, can you hear us?"

"Is he okay?" I asked, rubbing both eyes.

"I think he's OD'ing," Leo said softly, almost as if he regretted the words as they left his mouth.

"What?" Suddenly, I was sober as a judge, my body snapping into action. Was he joking? I reached for his neck, checking for a pulse like they'd shown us in health class. His body was like fire, his chest rising and falling with erratic breaths. "He can't be. How much did he take?"

No one seemed to have an answer. I reached for his shirt, trying to pull it over his head.

"Stop!" Henry said, grabbing my hand.

"He's burning up! Why are you all just standing there? We need to call 9-1-1! Did something happen? Did he hit his head?" I had no idea what to check for or check first; I only knew I had to keep moving. Keep doing. I couldn't sit still and watch him die.

"No," Piper said, tears streaming down her cheeks. "He just started shaking. And, like...foaming."

"It's an overdose," Henry said. "Leo's right. This is just like what happened with my brother."

"How much did he take?" I asked again.

"I have no idea," Piper cried, her voice a high-pitched whine.

"Okay. That's okay," I assured her. "It doesn't matter. Come on. I need you all to help me get him up. We're going to have to carry him to the car." I lifted his shoulders, slid my arms under his, and strained to pull him off the ground, my feet digging into the dirt.

Piper bent down next to me, shoving her arms under his back to help. I tugged with all my might, letting out a groan as my muscles used every spare ounce of power they had, but he barely budged. I wasn't strong enough. On my own, I didn't stand a chance of moving him. I stared up at the rest of the group.

"What are you waiting for? *Help me!*" I begged.

Leo sighed, but reached for Tyler's legs hesitantly, scooping him up at his knees. He stared into the distance, at the journey ahead of us, with a scowl. "I don't know. I don't think we can make it. It's too far."

"What are you talking about? We don't have a choice. We have to try," I insisted, lifting him again without warning as if to prove the point. My feet slid out from under me in an instant and I collapsed onto the forest floor, gasping for air. Tyler's back hit the ground with a *thud*.

"You're going to hurt him!" Piper shouted, her voice muddled with sobs.

"She can't hurt him any worse," Henry said.

"Come on, what are you doing?" I asked Henry. "Why aren't you helping? Please! We're wasting time!"

Henry shook his head, folding his arms across his chest, his jaw tight. "Trying to help him is a waste of time. We can't save him. It's too late. He'll be dead before we get him out of the woods."

"What are you talking about? We can't just give up. There's still time. There are five of us. If we work together, we'll—"

"*Still not make it.* You really think we can carry him all that way without getting hurt ourselves?" He jutted his head toward Lakynn, who was swaying in her spot drunkenly. "She's three sheets to the wind. The rest of us aren't much better. It's at least an hour to walk back to the cars, and that's under normal circumstances—"

"*We have to try,*" I argued, tugging Tyler up again. Filled with adrenaline, I dragged him a few feet across the forest floor, Piper and Leo attempting to keep up with me, before my arms burned for relief. My knees buckled underneath me and I crashed to the ground again, my stomach churning.

Leo cried out, unaware that I'd stopped, and fell sideways to avoid landing on top of me. When he hit the ground he shot up, grasping his ankle with both hands. "Shit! Fuck!"

"Be quiet!" Piper begged.

"Are you okay?" I asked, scrambling over Tyler with images of a protruding bone in my mind.

"I'm fine." He released his ankle gruffly. "I just twisted it." He tried to stand, wincing when he put weight on the foot. "I'll be fine."

"Are you sure?"

"Let's just go." He nodded toward Tyler again, but it was no use. With just the three of us, we'd never make it.

I turned my attention back to Henry. "Henry, *please?* Please just try. We're running out of time. What would you want us to do if it was you?"

He paused, his expression softening, if only slightly, and eventually, he nodded. "Fine." He glanced at Lakynn. "You good? Can you help?"

She nodded, squeezing her eyes shut and moving toward us with slow, cumbersome steps. Henry nudged me out of the way and scooped Tyler up from under his arms. Piper and I lifted together at his waist, and Lakynn helped Leo with his legs.

He was heavy, even with the five of us working together, and within moments, my entire body burned for relief. I locked my elbows, refusing to drop him. We just had to keep moving. It was the only way. Beside me, Leo was panting and wincing with each step, his eyes locked on Tyler with a stoic determination.

"Guys, I'm—" Piper let go of him, causing me to lurch forward from the strain of the extra weight, but the boys remained steady. She backed up seconds before she began to hurl the contents of her stomach onto the ground. The putrid smell of her vomit filled the air, and my stomach seized.

We froze. I couldn't bear to say anything as my eyes welled with tears. If I opened my mouth, I was going to be sick.

"*Ow, fu— Put him down,*" Leo shouted, and we dropped him again on command.

He crashed onto the ground, his foot colliding with Lakynn's. She yelped, hopping on the uninjured foot. "*Fucking ouch!*"

"What happened?" Henry asked.

"He landed on my foot!" she cried.

"You okay?"

She pressed her lips together, nodding slowly, her chin quivering.

"What happened to you, Leo?" Henry asked.

Leo was leaning over his knees, shaking his head adamantly. He rested all his weight on one leg, and lifted the cuff of his pants to examine his ankle. "I can't do it, guys. I... I think it might be broken. I can't—" He swiped a hand across the sweat gleaming on his forehead.

"We aren't going to make it," Henry said again, this time more firmly. He stepped back, wiping sweat from his temple.

"We can't give up on him," Piper begged, wiping her mouth with her arm as she turned back to us.

"We don't have any choice," Henry said. "I'm sorry. I wish there was another way. I really do. If we try to carry him, he'll be dead before we get there. And then what will we do?"

I tried to think, staring around at each of them. Piper was watching Henry, a gleam of resignation in her eyes. She was giving up. They all were.

"There has to be something. Maybe one of us can run ahead, drive into town, find someone who can help, and—"

"And what? Tell them we were out here partying and someone died?" Henry asked. "Is that really what you want us to do? I'm telling you, Beth, we can't save him. He'd be dead before they got back with help. All it would do is get us into trouble. He's not going to make it either way. Do any of us want our parents finding out what we were doing tonight? Do any of us want to be questioned by the cops? Or to go to jail?"

"Jail?" I scoffed. "We didn't kill him, but leaving him here...that *would* be killing him."

"And what about the drugs? What will your parents say when they find out about tonight? And yours?" He looked at Piper. "Because I know what mine will say. I'll never see the light of day again."

I waited for Piper's response, shaking my head slightly. I couldn't believe what I was hearing. Did any of that matter? Could they really be considering leaving him?

She hesitated, scraping her bottom lip with her top teeth. "I... I'm supposed to be home tonight. If my parents find out I snuck out, I'll be grounded for life."

"You guys... You're not being rational. This is a person's

life we're talking about. *Tyler's* life. He's a person. A kid, just like us."

Henry grabbed my shoulders. "And he brought the drugs, okay? The rest of us, we just brought alcohol. He was going to do the drugs with or without us. Is it our fault he took too much?" He shook me once.

"We can't just abandon him," I said softly, silently begging him to see reason.

His jaw was firm. He broke eye contact with me. "We don't have a choice. We have to leave him. We have to take our stuff and make it look like we were never here. It'll take us at least an hour to make it to our cars walking through the woods at night and another hour to get into town and find a pay phone or make it to the police station. There's nothing we can do for him now. I'm trying to save the rest of us."

I shook my head, wanting to fight, to argue, to call them all insane, but I was outnumbered. What if Henry was right? Tyler's seizing had already stopped and his breathing was slowing. Maybe we wouldn't make it in time. What would happen then? And, worse, what if the police thought we had something to do with it? What if they blamed us? What if we went to jail? What had seemed impossible only moments ago now seemed almost likely. I could never tell my parents we'd been doing drugs or drinking. My father was a judge, for crying out loud. This would kill him. *He* would kill *me*. My parents would never forgive me for anything like this. They'd disown me.

"Fine," I said with a groan, my pulse pounding in my ears. "But we have to move him. They can't find him here. There are cans and bottles from us going back years. That's all DNA. It will lead them straight to us."

"Okay." Henry huffed out a breath, looking around the woods. "But we aren't going to make it far. Where do you suggest we take him?" he asked, his hand still lingering on my arm.

I thought quickly, forcing myself to stay calm. This wasn't real. It was all a dream. I'd wake up tomorrow and realize it had all been a bad dream. "We should take him farther out in the woods. As far as we can carry him. We'll drag him if we have to. There's a small ravine with a stream. We'll leave him next to it. A hunter or someone will find him in a few days. By then, the water will have washed off any evidence we were with him."

Or maybe, if we were lucky, no one would ever find him at all.

AFTER JUST A FEW minutes of debate, which started with Piper saying it would be impossible for us to even carry him that far, especially with half the group injured and most of the group wasted in the dark woods on an unfamiliar path, and ended with Henry telling us it was what we were going to do regardless, we set to work.

I forced the reality of our situation out of my head as we lifted his body, vowing never to drink again if we just managed to get out of this mess.

Of course, Piper had been right. Our plan was dangerous and stupid. We were all drunk and most of us were high. We didn't know this part of the woods and couldn't see much in the darkness, so we tripped over tree roots and rocks on several occasions and dropped him more than once. No longer working under the pressure of trying to keep him alive, we were able to pace ourselves better. We stopped every few moments to rest, panting and exhausted before we'd even made it out of sight of the clearing.

My body shook with adrenaline, fear, and pain. Every step, every movement, was torture and he seemed to only get heavier as we went. I could smell the vomit on Piper's breath across from me, and it was everything I could do not to vomit myself.

We heard the sound of the water before we saw it. We'd made it less than a mile away from the clearing, but it had taken us what felt like hours to do so. As much as it pained me to admit it, I had to accept the fact that we'd never have been able to make the nearly four-mile trek back to the cars in time. Henry had been right about everything.

When the ravine finally came into view, every muscle in my body screamed for relief. We laid him down with his feet in the water, and I felt for a pulse again. He was cool to the touch already, his pulse barely there.

"He's almost gone," I whispered with tears welling in my eyes. I brushed them away, sinking down on the dirt next to him. We sat with him for a moment, our heads hung in silence as I waited until I could no longer feel his pulse.

I nodded, unable to bring myself to say the words, but everyone seemed to understand. Piper let out a wail so gut wrenching I had to turn away from her so she wouldn't see my own tears.

I didn't completely understand why I was so upset. I didn't feel like I had any right to be. Tyler wasn't part of our group. Not really. But when he and Piper had become close during a school project, he'd begun tagging along when we hung out and showing up with her to our bonfires. Not too long after that, they'd begun dating. It wasn't like we were best friends, but I was shocked to realize how much I cared about him.

Don't get me wrong, I wasn't a monster. I knew it would hurt to lose him, like it would hurt to lose any of our classmates, but this was different. Though I didn't understand it until that moment, Tyler *was* one of us.

His loss was one we'd carry with us.

I didn't fully realize that until we stood to leave him. None of us would ever be the same after that night. Whoever we'd been walking into those woods, those kids were gone. I knew that. I understood it somewhere deep in my bones.

This loss, this secret... It was one we had to take with us to our graves.

No one could ever know what had happened that night in the woods. No one but the five of us.

We swore it to each other as we left him and walked away—forever connected by what we'd done.

Then we headed back to the bonfire to clean up the evidence from that night. When we were finished, we walked away from our secret place, knowing we'd never be able to go back there again. I cried as we walked, letting the tears fall silently as the leaves crunched underfoot. It was the only place I felt safe anymore, and now, it was gone. It was another loss, one I felt almost as deeply as Tyler's.

TYLER DIDN'T HAVE A CAR, something I only remembered an hour later, when we made it to our cars to leave. He always rode with Piper, which was the one bit of mercy the universe showed us that night. A car would've been the final piece of evidence to tie us to him. I was tired and sore and desperately didn't want to think about disposing of a vehicle after all we'd been through.

I just wanted to go home and shower off the guilt I felt.

We said solemn goodbyes that night and separated to our vehicles, which were parked along the side of the highway. As I shut the door of my car, I rested my head on the steering wheel, hot tears falling down my cheeks.

How had this happened?

How had so much changed so fast?

Hours ago, we walked into the woods as carefree kids. Now...were we murderers? I mean, it wasn't like we killed him, but we didn't *help* him, either.

I was too young to go to jail. I had plans for my life. Dreams. Goals.

Tyler had those, too.

I forced the thought away.

No. Tyler was a junkie who was probably never going to make anything of himself anyway.

And now he was dead. That was that.

The vile thoughts were painful to think, but the alternative was worse. I couldn't allow myself to believe anything else. It was his own fault. I had to believe that or I'd never be able to live with myself. Henry was right. He'd brought the drugs. No one forced him to take them.

We had no choice.

We had no choice.

We had no choice.

I wiped the tears from my cheeks aggressively, inhaling deeply. I needed to pull it together.

I turned the key in my ignition.

Tick

Tick

Tick

The lights on my dash came on, but nothing else happened. I turned it again.

Tick

Tick

Tick

Fuck. Anything else wanna go wrong tonight?

I slammed my hands on the steering wheel. The battery was dead. It was happening more and more often with this car. I looked around, checking my rearview.

Everyone had already left.

Everyone except Henry, who was still parked behind me.

Was it wishful thinking to hope he was making sure I made it out okay?

I opened the car door and stepped outside. His face was buried in his steering wheel and, as I got closer, I felt fear creeping in. I knocked on his window apprehensively, and he jolted, swiping his cheeks. His eyes were weary and bloodshot.

Not dead.

Just crying.

He rolled his window down slowly. "Yeah?"

"Sorry... Um, my car won't start again. Do you still have jumper cables?"

He sniffled, wiping his nose with the back of his arm.

"Sure thing." I stepped back as he pushed the door open and walked around to the trunk of his car. He popped it open and grabbed the cables, then handed them to me. "Here, let me move up there." I waited as he pulled his car in front of mine.

He worked in silence, and I did my best to keep out of the way. Once he'd finished and my car was running, he placed the cables back in his trunk.

I followed him. "Thank you."

He nodded absentmindedly. "You should leave it running for a while to charge. You really need to get a new battery."

"I know. My mom's supposed to be asking my dad, but..." I trailed off, not wanting to go into it. "Anyway, I'm sorry you have to keep doing this. The other day after school, I asked Lakynn, but she didn't have any cables."

"I know. I actually bought her some last year, but she never has them with her. It's fine. I don't mind it, I'd just hate to think of what would've happened if I left before you realized it was dead."

So, maybe he was waiting for me.

"Me too. So, yeah, thanks...for everything."

He gave a stiff nod. "Thanks for siding with me back there."

"You were right," I said with a shrug.

"I wish I wasn't." He sniffled, swiping his cheek with his shoulder.

"I know this must make you think of your brother." Was it wrong to bring that up? I couldn't tell what was wrong or right anymore.

He nodded. "I'm fine. It just sucks."

"It's okay, you know?"

He met my eyes finally. "What's okay?"

"It's okay *not* to be fine sometimes. Especially after what we just went through."

He reached out his hands gently, brushing my fingers with his.

"Come here," I said, holding out my arms for him. He fell into them, not crying, but just allowing me to hold some of his weight for a second.

"I hate this," he said, his breath hot on my neck.

"I do, too," I admitted.

He pulled back, but not far, so our faces were just inches apart. "I'm sorry I hurt you."

"I know," I said, nodding. Bitter tears stung my eyes.

"I do care about you. You know that. And...if Lakynn hadn't wanted to get back together, who knows?"

"It's fine," I said stiffly. "I should go. I can't do this right now." I turned to walk away, but he took hold of my arm, stopping me in my tracks.

"I meant what I said to you that night."

I couldn't bear to meet his eyes.

"Look at me," he begged.

"Why? Why do I have to look at you, Henry? To make it all hurt worse? You asked me not to tell Lakynn what happened, and I haven't. You asked me to pretend like everything was normal, and I have. I've done everything you asked, but don't torture me like this."

He rested his forehead against mine. "You think this isn't torture for me?"

"It didn't look like it tonight."

He rolled his eyes, frowning as he fought back tears. His

chin wrinkled, lips pressed together to form a thin line. "Well, we all know I'm a good actor."

I reached up, brushing a tear from his cheek almost involuntarily.

He stopped my hand, moving it to his lips. "It's torture wanting you so badly and not being able to have you."

I pulled away. "That was *your* choice!"

"I wasn't given a choice. How could we ever tell Lakynn about us?" The way he said *us* sent a pang of sadness through me. There was no us anymore. He'd made that clear.

"You were broken up when it happened! She broke up with you."

"And she wanted to get back together the next day. How could I tell her about us? It would break her heart, ruin your friendship..."

"So what are you saying, Henry? What do you want?"

"I want you both," he said through gritted teeth. "I don't know what I want. And that's not fair to either of you."

"What happened between us shouldn't have happened," I told him dismissively, arms folded across my chest. "You called me because you needed a friend, and Leo's no use at these sorts of things. You were vulnerable."

His brows drew down. "Do you think that's why I kissed you? Because I was vulnerable?" His eyes filled with a passion like I'd only seen in movies.

"I mean—"

He gripped both my cheeks, lowering his mouth until it was just inches from mine. "That has nothing to do with it. I kissed you because I wanted to. Simple as that."

"How is th—" He pressed his lips to mine, cutting me off, and just like that, we were back in his bedroom, my belly full of butterflies as his hands explored my bare skin, our bodies slick with sweat. My head pounded with adrenaline, body on fire with anticipation. Was it going to happen again? It couldn't. What about...

His hand slipped behind my head, cradling it gently. He nipped at my lips.

"We shouldn't do this..." I whispered breathlessly.

"Because you don't want to?" he asked, resting his forehead against mine again, our lips brushing with each word.

It took me a moment to answer. I had to close my eyes to do it. I couldn't bear to turn him down while I was staring into those eyes. "I don't want her to get hurt."

"I don't want that, either." Despite saying that, he kissed me again, the air closing in around us and expanding as real as a heartbeat. Nothing else existed. Nothing else mattered. I couldn't summon the will to pull away, even if I'd wanted to. Instead, I let him lead me to his car. He pulled open the door and slid the seat back, only tearing our lips apart for milliseconds at a time as he eased himself down and pulled me on top of him.

Anyone could've caught us, but I couldn't bring myself to care.

Not about our parents.

Not about Lakynn.

Not about anything but the way his kiss felt. He pulled his shirt off, then mine, trailing kisses along my cheek, then down my neck, and onto my collarbone.

Within seconds, my bra was off and he flung it into the passenger seat. Goose bumps lined my skin. This was crossing a line we'd never crossed. If we went through with this, we were cheating.

He was cheating.

I was betraying the closest friend I'd ever had.

He unbuttoned my pants, and I didn't stop him. Didn't want to stop him. His hand slipped between my legs. My body tensed with pleasure, everything else in the world forgotten, even if just for the moment.

IT WASN'T until he was inside me, the seat laid all the way back, windows completely fogged over, that I heard someone outside of the car. I froze, jumping off of him so fast I accidentally kneed him between the legs.

He doubled over. "What the fu—"

"Someone's outside the car." I pulled my shirt over my head quickly, searching for my pants.

"What are you talking about? Get back over here."

"*Stop it!*" I hissed. "I'm serious. I heard something."

"What was it?" Sensing my panic, he pulled his pants up, buttoning them quickly.

"It sounded like someone said my name."

He relaxed, giving me a dubious look. "Uh, yeah. That would've been me."

I slapped his chest. "I'm serious. Someone's—"

"Henry?" The voice was zombie-like, low and gruff. I recognized it immediately.

"What the fuck?" He opened the car door, stepping out. Tyler was there, just outside the car and drenched. "T-Tyler? You're... You're okay?"

"I don't know. I... I don't feel good."

"Yeah, buddy..." Henry spoke slowly. The fog on the

windows was beginning to clear with the door standing open. Tiny, clear specks splattered the windshield like stars. I finished pulling my pants on, my fingers trembling. Had Tyler heard us? He was too out of it, wasn't he? But what if he wasn't? What if he told someone what we did? Worse, what if he remembered what we'd done in the woods? What if he knew we left him? "Listen, you wandered off out there. We couldn't find you. Are you okay?"

"I, um…" He sounded weak. "I don't remember. I must've gone to…to take a leak or something. Then I woke up in this, like…stream. I'm fucking freezing, man," he said with a laugh. "Do you have a towel or anything? Some dry clothes, maybe?"

"Nah, I don't."

"Oh." He was quiet for a moment. "Listen, can I catch a ride? Piper must've ditched."

Henry spoke quickly as I searched for somewhere to hide. There was nowhere. "Uh, well, we were all heading out. I think Piper thought you must've walked somewhere else or something. I can give you a ride, but can you check back in the woods and see if you see Beth anywhere? I was waiting for her to pee. So, if you'll just check over there and — *No! Wait, wait!*" He was too late.

Tyler swung open the passenger door and stared down at me—shirt inside out, one shoe missing, hair a mess, still reeking of sex. I saw him register the foggy windows, then my car, and a wicked smile formed on his lips.

"*Well, well, well… Found her.*"

"Tyler, look, I can explain—"

"Explain what?" he asked, feigning ignorance with an

exaggerated frown on his lips. "Explain why you're here, half-dressed, with your girlfriend's best friend?"

"Yeah, um, that," Henry said. "Listen, it's not what it looks like."

"He was helping me," I told him, leaping from the car. "My battery died and—"

"Yeah, it really looks like he was helping you a lot." He grabbed hold of a wad of my messy hair, pulling me to his chest. His clothes were icy cold and sopping wet. I shivered instantly. "We could all use some help like that."

"Let me go!" I recoiled, and he let out a laugh that turned into a cough. His breath reeked of booze.

"Don't fuckin' touch her," Henry shouted, rushing toward us. For a moment, I worried the worst would happen. I could see the anger in Tyler's eyes. And the desire.

What would he do to me?

Would Henry be able to stop him?

He released my hair and wiped his mouth with his arm, then clicked his tongue and turned away from me. "On second thought, it's a nice night. I think I'll walk." There was an arrogance to his demeanor that hadn't been there before.

"What? Where are you going?" Henry shouted after him.

"She deserves better than you," Tyler said, then grumbled under his breath. For a moment, I felt my chest fill with a bit of pride, but then I heard, "Both of you."

Lakynn.

He wasn't talking about me.

He meant Lakynn.

He was going to tell her.

I'd always suspected Tyler had a thing for Lakynn, though we all knew he never stood a chance with her.

"You have no idea what you're talking about," Henry shouted after him.

Without looking back, he said, "Guess we'll have to let her decide that, won't we?"

Before I knew what was happening, Henry launched forward. He was faster than Tyler, likely stronger too, but it didn't matter. Tyler never saw it coming. Henry placed both hands on his back, shoving him forward with all his might.

As quickly as it happened, it was over. Tyler fell without enough warning to even try to break the fall. He only emitted a small scream the moment before he hit the ground. He landed face-first on the pavement with a sickening crunch.

No.

No.

No.

We stood silently for a moment, both of us still processing what had happened.

"What did you do?" I asked with utter disbelief from several feet back. Moments ago, we'd regained our freedom and our innocence, but just like that, it was snatched away once again.

Henry turned to look at me, true horror in his eyes. "He was going to..." He stared at his trembling hands in shock. "I-I couldn't let him tell her."

"He was alive, Hen. We could finally take back what we did. He didn't remember anything." I stepped forward cautiously as a dark pool of what I knew would be blood formed around his head.

"If we let him go, if we let him live, he would've told Lakynn everything. Do you think she would've ever forgiven us?" His hands were balled into fists, and he looked as though he was trying to convince himself as much as me.

"We didn't have to do this. We could've talked to him. Made up an excuse. Figured something out. *Anything* out. He didn't have to die."

"No." He grabbed my shoulders as I started to sink to the ground. "He did. He did have to die. He was dangerous. He was going to hurt you."

"He was walking away!" I shouted.

"Sure. For now he was. But what would happen if he came back? When I wasn't around? What if I wasn't here to protect you?"

"You don't know that that would've happened! You don't know if he would've—"

"*I couldn't—*" he shouted, then lowered his voice, "I couldn't take that chance. Not with you. Not with Lakynn. Not with any of us. I protected us all, don't you see that? Because he might not have remembered what we did today, but what if he woke up tomorrow and remembered? What if he told everyone what we did? Our parents? We'd lose everyone, Beth. And, even if he didn't ever remember that we hid his body, we'd lose everyone that matters the second he told Lakynn what we just did."

"You don't know that."

"Oh, I do. I do know that, and you do too. You've seen the way he looks at her." He spoke through gritted teeth.

The contents of my stomach curdled. "Is...is that what this was about? Did you do this *on purpose*? Did you want him dead?"

He scowled, spinning away from me. "Of course not. Don't be ridiculous."

I covered my mouth in horror and disbelief, trying to calm myself down. I didn't know what to believe. I trusted Henry, loved him, even. But what I'd just seen... I wasn't sure I could ever forget it. He felt like a stranger to me. "What now, then? We can't carry him back out there by ourselves."

"Let me think." He rubbed his forehead aggressively, swiping his hand through his hair.

"Oh, now you want to think? A rational thought a few seconds ago could've saved a life."

"Don't point fingers at me. We wouldn't even be in this mess if you'd been able to tell us he wasn't actually dead back there."

"I couldn't feel a pulse. I'm not a trained professional, Henry. I was terrified and shaking and had no idea what was happening. If he was overdosing, maybe the cold water in the spring woke him up. Don't blame me for this."

"*I'm not blaming anyone,*" he shouted, then lowered his voice again. "I'm just trying to get us out of this mess." He started pacing then.

I stood there, my body trembling with fury. Fury at him for what he'd done. Fury at myself for allowing it to happen. Finally, I said, "We need to move him. This road isn't busy, but if someone happens to come down it and they see him here, we're done for."

He stopped in his tracks, as if something had just occurred to him, and nodded. "I've got an idea. Help me get him in the trunk of my car."

An hour later, we pulled into the marina by Lake Alton. We drove through the parking lot slowly, keeping an eye out for anyone else there, but to my relief, at this time of night, the place was a ghost town.

"So, what's your plan? What are we doing here?" I asked as we slowed to a stop in front of a group of boat slips. The whole way over, he wouldn't tell me anything. He just kept saying I should trust him, though I was having a hard time doing that. He wasn't acting like the Henry I knew right then.

"Number 238," he said, pointing straight ahead. "It's my parents' boat slip. We'll get on the boat and take him out into the lake."

"Are you crazy? Someone will see."

"There's no one here," he said, stepping out of the car. "Trust me. These boats are all owned by people just like my parents. Do you know how often we use this thing? Hardly ever, and definitely not at night. No one's out here. We'll put him below deck, stop when there's no one around, and dump the body."

"I don't know. Shouldn't we just go to the police? Maybe we can explain—"

"There's nothing to explain." He grabbed my arm. "Right now, you're either with me or against me. If I go down, we all do. This is the only way to save yourself, Beth. The only way to save us all."

And so, I did.

Like everything Henry had ever asked of me, I agreed.

After it was over, we never spoke of that night again.

CHAPTER TWENTY-EIGHT

LAKYNN

Present Day

I stared at my husband and best friend in disbelief. "So, wait...y-you..." I paused, pressing my fingers to the bridge of my nose. "You guys had sex that night? After we'd *killed* someone? While we were dating?"

"We hadn't killed him," Henry said.

"You didn't know that when you were fu—"

"It was a mistake," Bethany said, cutting me off. "I'm so sorry, Lake. Believe me when I say that it has eaten me up every day of my life. I hate myself for ever being so stupid." I rolled my eyes, turning away from her.

"How many times?"

They exchanged a look. "How many..."

"Times," I said again, looking directly at Bethany. "How many times did you have sex with my husband?"

"Well, twice. But once when you were broken up, and then once when you'd just gotten back together. Never again

209

after that night," Bethany said. "It was a mistake. An awful mistake. And I understand if you can never forgive us, but—"

"Babe." Henry moved forward, putting a hand on my shoulder. "It was twenty-five years ago. I should've told you, but it meant nothing. To either of us."

Bethany shook her head in agreement. "It really didn't."

"It's not like either of us were virgins when we got together and—"

"This isn't about that," I snapped. "This is about you sleeping with my best friend behind my back and keeping it a secret for twenty-five years. What? Have the two of you been laughing about it when I leave the room? *Ha ha, there goes stupid, clueless Lakynn."*

"Of course not," Henry said, his expression sincere. "I love you, Lakynn. *You.* I would never do that to you."

"I wouldn't, either. We've never even talked about it. It's the worst thing either of us have ever done," Bethany said.

"You mean besides the murder," I said, my head fuzzy with all I was learning. They exchanged glances and nodded, their faces riddled with guilt. "Well, you'll forgive me if I don't take you at your word right now," I sneered at them both, crossing my arms. I began to pace for fear I might fall over if I didn't. "Do you two want to be together?"

"No!" they said at the same time, equal parts horror and shock in their voices.

"Are you sure?"

"I only want you, Lakynn. I've only wanted you. I've never been unfaithful to you aside from that night. Not before and not after. You're the love of my life," Henry said, reaching for my hand. I kept pacing.

"Does Leo know?"

Henry looked at Beth, who folded her arms across her chest and tucked her chin. "No. But he will. I'm going to tell him after this. As soon as we find him."

"You'd better. Or I will," I said firmly. She nodded. I sucked in a breath. "Is there anything else I should know?"

"That's all," Bethany said firmly. "And I'll answer any questions and tell you anything you want to know, but that's really it."

Shane had backed away from us, and when I turned around, I saw him gripping the wall for support. "You guys are talking about murdering an innocent person, and you're more worried about them cheating on you?" He shook his head. "Is this a joke? Is this some sort of prank?"

"It's not a prank," Henry said. "We were dumb kids. It was a mistake, like we said. We were all teenagers once, right?"

"Sure," Shane said. "And teenagers might knock over a mailbox or egg someone's house. They don't murder people and dump their bodies in a lake."

"Okay." Bethany put up a hand. "I know. And if you want to turn us in, we won't stop you. I know we've told you a lot here, and I'm sorry you've had to hear it, but if this really is the only way to get out, then that's what we have to do."

Shane didn't say anything, but kept his distance anyway.

"But if that was all we had to do, why aren't they letting us out?" Henry asked, staring around the room thoughtfully.

"Because there's one more secret," I said. "Mine." I turned my note over, reading it again. "I thought this was originally about us telling Shane what we've done, but now

I'm realizing my secret is supposed to be shared with you, Henry."

He squared his shoulders to me, bracing himself. "Whatever you need to tell me, I can handle it. I love you."

I'd kept the secret quiet for so long for fear of hurting him, but now, I was going to relish in his pain, if only for a moment. "When I broke up with you the week before everything happened, it was because I slept with Tyler and I couldn't bear the guilt." I stared at him, unblinking, willing myself to keep a stony face.

"You...you what?" He cocked his head to the side.

"I slept with Tyler. It was that night you couldn't come to the bonfire. One of the first nights Piper brought him, before they were dating. We were drinking and...and, well, it just sort of happened."

"You were really trying to guilt-trip me just now when you did the exact same thing?" he asked, a muscle in his neck twitching.

"*It's not the exact same thing*," I said firmly, jabbing a finger in the air at him. "Tyler wasn't your best friend. He wasn't even your friend. And you haven't been hanging out with Tyler, inviting him to our house every day for the past twenty-five years while we kept our dirty little secret behind your back. Tyler wasn't in our wedding. Tyler doesn't pick up our kids from school." I was shouting then, unable to keep my fury at bay. "This has very little to do with you two having sex nearly three decades ago and everything to do with the fact that you both kept it from me every single day since then. So, you want my confession? There you go, I did it too." My hands went up to my sides. "We were stupid kids, like you said, but I *never* would've treated either of you this way. You can't blame this mistake on us being stupid teenagers. Grow the hell up." I spun on my heel, moving farther away from them.

As I neared the door, I froze.

Listening.

Down the hall, someone had broken into a faint, slow clap.

CHAPTER TWENTY-NINE

BETHANY

S hane stepped out into the hall first. Probably thinking nothing out there could be worse than the room he was currently in with us. I couldn't blame him, really.

"*You?*" he asked, his footsteps moving quicker. As we made our way into the hall, the fight momentarily forgotten, I gasped at the sight of the man waiting for us in the kitchen.

Penn.

"Yes, me," he said plainly. "Who else?"

"Where's Etta?" Lakynn asked him.

"Etta isn't part of this," Penn said with a casual flick of his wrist. "This is between us."

"What is?" Henry asked, his voice firm. He stepped in front of Lakynn and me protectively.

Penn chuckled, moving around to the other side of the bar and pouring a drink. "Would anyone care for a drink?"

"Where's Leo?" I asked, my voice trembling.

"How should I know?" he asked with a shrug.

Rage bubbled in my stomach. I bit down so hard a pain shot through my jaw.

"Penn, what in the hell is going on? Where are our friends? Why are you doing this?" Lakynn asked.

"You mean you don't recognize me?" His voice was different then, deeper and gruffer than it had been before. It *did* sound familiar. "I've gained a bit of weight. Packed on some muscle. Got off the drugs. Cut my hair. Stopped wearing that god-awful eyeliner. Got rich." He rolled his eyes. "What am I forgetting here? Oh, right...aged twenty-five years."

I gasped, taking a step back. *No.* "Tyler?"

"That's right." He took a sip of his wine and chuckled. "*What?* Were you expecting to find me at the bottom of a lake? Well, it seems like I just can't die, can I?"

"How?" was all Henry managed to croak.

"Well, as it turns out, I'm a pretty good swimmer. And you're not that strong a fighter. You knocked me out for a while, but the next thing I remember is waking up in the trunk of a moving car. I realized then what was happening. It took me a while, but it was a long car ride, and I finally figured out why I woke up at first so deep in the woods. I remembered you shoving me down on the road that night. And I finally understood that you wanted to get rid of me."

His mouth curved into a bitter, haunted smile. "So, I had to come up with a plan quickly. I knew my best bet was to let you think you'd gotten away with it. I wanted you to leave me somewhere, thinking I was dead, so I could run away again. This time, I wouldn't go running straight for the very people trying to hurt me. So, I lay perfectly still, which wasn't hard to do after nearly overdosing and having a concussion within a few hours of each other. Imagine my shock when I found myself on a boat. I thought about trying to fight you, but let's be honest, I wasn't exactly my best that night. There was only one choice. So, as soon as you dropped me in the water, I started swimming."

"It's not possible," I said, shaking my head.

"Why now? Why wouldn't you come back to us right away? In public, if you were worried about your safety?" Lakynn asked.

"Why not go to the police?" Shane asked.

"You'd think it would be that simple, wouldn't you?" he asked with a dry laugh. "No, see, I did go to the police."

"You did?" My jaw dropped. "When?"

Had he been recording us this whole time?

Was that why he wanted our confession?

"The next day. Once I'd made it to shore and slept enough to get my strength back. I went straight to the police." He slapped the counter. "And do you want to know what they told me?"

We were silent. Waiting.

"They told me that there was no way they'd be able to convict you because I was accusing the daughter of a judge" —he pointed to me—"the daughter of a lawyer"—pointed to Lakynn—"the son of one of the most wealthy families in Poe" —pointed to Henry—"the daughter of the superintendent, and the son of the head of city council. In other words, Poe royalty. That's right... You were *rich*. Well-to-do. And I was not. And the cops made it very clear that day. And, to add to it, they said the drugs wouldn't look good on me since it would make it look like I'd been supplying drugs to minors.

They said if I pursued it, your families could press charges against me."

"You were in our grade..." Lakynn said softly.

"I was eighteen, and most of you were still seventeen. But it didn't matter. They'd made up their minds. They didn't believe me. Said it sounded like we'd had a wild night and wild dreams, and sent me on my way. It was my word against all of yours, and I didn't need a jury to tell me who they'd side with."

Lakynn sucked in a breath. "Penn, er, um, Tyler, look I'm so—"

He wrinkled his nose with disgust. "Sorry? Are you sorry? I bet you are now. Back then, you thought you'd all gotten away with it. I guess you had. Meanwhile, my own parents didn't believe me. They said you'd never hang around with someone like me." He looked away, jaw tight. "They moved us away shortly after that, worried I'd end up embarrassing them more, I guess. I finished high school in Georgia. I got married. Built a life. Built a company. But no matter what I did, I could never forget about you all and what you did to me."

"Tyler," Lakynn went on, "I know this doesn't make it okay, but we *are* sorry. We all regret what we did to you. We were stupid kids, but that's no excuse. We were scared that night, and...we've regretted it every day since. I mean, our lives may look good from the outside, but if you've been listening all night, you've heard what a mess we are. Leo has a drug problem. The secret ruined Piper's marriage. It's weighed heavily on us all for years now."

He narrowed his gaze at her. "Well, you'll have to forgive me if that doesn't make it all better. I really thought we had something, Lakynn. I thought you cared about me. But in the end, I never stood a chance, did I? It was always him." He jutted a chin toward Henry.

Lakynn tucked her chin to her chest. "I'm so sorry," she whispered.

Tyler smacked a palm on the counter, a defiant look in his eyes. "And I'm sorry for what I have to do next."

"What are you going to do?" Henry asked. "Are you going to kill us? What was the point of all of that? What do you want, man?"

"Where is Piper?" Shane asked from the back of the room.

"Questions, questions, so many questions," he sang, refilling his glass of wine as he bounced his head back and forth. "Which one should I answer first?" He walked around the counter and sat down on a barstool, one leg over the other. "How about what I want, which is the truth."

"We've already confessed," I said.

"To me, yes. But I'm going to need that confession for the police."

"Why? You've obviously done okay for yourself. What good does it do now?" Henry asked. "We have lives, man. Kids. Innocent kids. You can't do this."

"I can, and I will. Either with your help or by force."

"Meaning what?"

"Meaning, if you don't go to the police, I'll kill you all."

With that, as the words were still leaving his mouth, the house went dark once again.

CHAPTER THIRTY

LAKYNN

Someone grabbed hold of my waist, shoving me forward. *"Let go of m—"* I tried to fight them off, but a hand clamped over my mouth. I was shoved into someone else, then into a wall as the hand left my mouth. I ran my fingers along the wall, trying to figure out where I was.

Was this the living room? Or had I made it into the dining room somehow?

There was a wall behind me made of pure concrete. With one hand on the wall, I reached the other out, stretching my fingers in hopes of connecting with something.

A gust of wind smacked my face and someone else slammed into me, knocking me backward. *"Ouch!"* I shouted.

"Lake?" came the whispered voice.

"Beth?" My anger toward my best friend momentarily dissipated as I engulfed her in a hug for what I knew might be the last time.

"I'm so sorry, I'm so sorry..." she whispered in my ear.

"Shhh... Not now," I quieted her. I hugged her tight, my voice caught in my throat. I couldn't bring myself to say more and had no idea what I wanted to say anyway.

Someone tugged on my arm, and I assumed it was her. "Where are we going?" I whispered.

The voice that replied wasn't Bethany's. "Come on."

"What?"

"Who was that?" Bethany asked.

Just then, a light flipped on. Bright, white, and blinding.

These lights weren't the ordinary fluorescents from the house, but rather the bright LEDs that reminded me of a surgical unit. I stared around, blinking rapidly as I tried to understand what we were seeing.

Concrete on every side of us. Henry was there. Shane, too.

And—

"*Leo?*" Bethany shouted, launching herself into her husband's arms. "Oh my god, I thought you were... I thought..." She kissed him square on the lips, tears glistening on her cheeks.

"Shh!" Henry warned.

"It's okay. No one can hear us in here." I recognized Piper's voice before I saw her.

Shane rushed across the room, scooping her into his arms. "I was so worried about you."

"I'm sorry," she told him, burying her face in his chest.

"Where have you guys been?" Bethany asked, resting her head on Leo's shoulder, both arms still around him. "Where are we?"

"We're in the tunnels Henry talked about earlier," Piper said.

"But how did you find them?" I asked, taking in every inch of the space. It seemed to go on for miles in either direction, the full length of the house at least. "Are we underground?"

"Not here, but if you go down those stairs, you will be," came another voice. One I didn't immediately recognize. When I turned around, my heart filled with a strange mixture of joy and confusion.

"Tom? Eleanor? Oh my god!"

Our old neighbors stood in front of us, dressed all in black. Tom had a gash on his forehead with a dried bloodstain that stretched down into his bushy gray eyebrow. "You're hurt." I reached for him.

He waved off my concern. "Oh, I'm all right. Just a bump."

"That's more than a bump. You need stitches," Bethany said, examining him closer.

"We'll worry about that once we get the six of you out of here and safe," he said, nudging us forward. "Come on, we need to get farther underground."

"I don't understand," Henry said, stopping us. "I thought you moved away. How are you here right now?"

"Well, we did move," Eleanor said, giving her husband a doting smile. "But just down the road."

"So how are you here?" Henry repeated.

"It's a long story," Leo said.

"So, tell us," Henry prompted.

"We will," Tom said, taking another step in the direction of the stairs. "But let's keep moving. I'm trying to find you a way out." He led us down the stairs, our footsteps echoing in the quiet rooms, and down a long, well-lit hall.

"Can you tell us while we walk?" I asked, when Tom stopped to look down two separate halls.

He appeared conflicted. "Well, first, I guess I should apologize. I never meant for anyone to get hurt or to put you in harm's way at all. Tonight was supposed to be fun. I never thought Tyler would—"

"Wait a second, you're behind this? And you know Tyler?" I asked, not sure which I should be more concerned about.

"Well, not all of it, no," Eleanor said.

"Tyler's our nephew," Tom said. "We were just trying to help him by offering him a job."

I swiped my palms across my dress, eyes darting between Tom and Eleanor. They'd never been anything but kind to us, but could we trust them? Knowing what we knew? What if they were helping him?

"A job?"

Tom stopped, a small smile filling his lips. "Yes. Working for us. I had this new business idea, you see. Er, well, it's not *new*, but it's a combination of two things that have never been combined before. You've heard of the escape rooms, I'm assuming. Our grandkids say they're all the rage now. And then, we thought, well, we've always loved a good murder mystery dinner. So"—he looked to Eleanor for support and she touched his arm gently—"we thought, why not combine the two? We could charge tickets for people to come to our house and we'd have it all rigged up, start with a nice, elegant dinner and dessert, and then they'd move on to riddles and clues throughout the night to get them out in a specific amount of time. You all were meant to be our first customers."

"Like a trial run," Eleanor said, as if it needed further explanation.

"But...Tom, for those to work, you have to get permission from the people playing," Henry pointed out.

"Yes, well, I thought we had your permission." He sounded exasperated.

"Tyler told him he'd sent us invitations explaining it all and we'd said yes," Piper said, filling in the blanks.

"And all the secrets and lies stuff was Tyler. Tom and Eleanor only placed the regular clues—the riddle about the rug, and the key that led to the blocks you all had to put together, plus the pirate riddle and the key hidden near the eye, and the eight o'clock clue. Once you turned the lights back on, it was supposed to be over," Leo added.

"Yes. We hired Mrs. Doyle to bring you dinner and dessert, then lock the doors and leave you on your own for the games. We'd be monitoring everything the entire time from the control room upstairs. Of course, this was just a trial run, to work out the kinks. The actual event would be much, much longer," Tom added, nodding. "With better riddles and branded clues. We just wanted to get your feedback on what worked before we ordered everything." His expression was that of a puppy waiting to get scolded.

"We talked to the city and got the zoning approvals. It was why we had the wall installed around the yard, and all the security. The whole house is wired. We can control every door, every light switch, every fan, everything in the house with a controller upstairs. The company Tyler owns can do all of that fancy stuff, so we offered him the job. We thought we were doing him a favor because his parents mentioned business has been slow. And he seemed so excited to come back here. He said they'd get it all installed and ready to go while we were away on vacation, and when we returned, it would be ready to go for the trial run. Like they said, he even agreed to do the invitations and tell you all what was going on," Eleanor said. "We had no idea about your history with him or that he harbored such a grudge. We never dreamed he'd try anything like this."

"When we came home last night, we worked together as a team to set everything up and Tyler gave me the mother-board controller back."

"At least, we thought he did," Eleanor said. "When we realized it wasn't working, he said it was because he wanted to handle everything, since he'd done all the work here." She paused. "We didn't see the harm in it, but I had a bad feeling about it. I started snooping and that's when I found all the recordings and pictures he'd had taken of you all."

"He'd been stalking us for years," Piper said. "Our phones, computers, everything... It's all bugged."

"I'm afraid it's true," Eleanor said. "And, well, we weren't going to let him get away with whatever his plan was. We know you kids aren't technically our family, but we've always thought of you like our kids. So, Tom told him in no uncertain terms that he had to leave, that the plan was off, and he was fired." She rolled her eyes as Tom pointed to the gash on his head. "Well, you can imagine how that went."

"He hit you?" I demanded.

Tom nodded.

"Then locked us in a room," Eleanor said.

"But he didn't know about the tunnel system. In fact, no one knows it exists except you guys. We never trusted anyone else with that secret," Tom said.

I couldn't bear to look at them, guilt weighing on me. "But you must not be able to trust us now? After all we did? Surely you've heard... He's your nephew. How can you try to help us if you know who we are and what we did to him?" I asked.

Tom's expression softened. "This isn't the way. What Tyler's doing isn't right. I don't believe we're defined by our worst moments, no matter how dark they are. We're defined by what we do after our worst moments. There's no doubt you did a very bad thing, but I am not the one who gets to judge you for that. I hope you've done enough good in your life to earn forgiveness—from yourself, and someday from him, too. But I don't get to dole out punishment for your crimes. No one but the law can do that. We had to save you, for our own conscience, but also because we care about you. It's like she said, we've always thought of you as our kids. What we've learned doesn't change that."

Bittersweet tears stung my eyes, and I shook my head.

"But then, I don't understand. You used the tunnels to save us?" Henry asked.

"That's right. We snuck into the tunnels from the room they locked us in and tried to keep an eye on what was going on. We don't think they realized we had escaped from the room until Leo went missing, and by then, they couldn't locate us anyway. We were trying to get to you all before the end of the game, to protect you, but it wasn't easy. There are cameras everywhere. We had all-black clothing prepared in case we had to move around in the dark to help with the game at all, and we could travel room to room via the tunnels, even with the doors locked, but even that came with risks. If he caught us on camera, in a flashlight glare or when the black light was on, I was scared of what he'd do to us all," Eleanor said.

"So, all the notes and blood and stuff, that was all Tyler?" I asked, drying my eyes.

Piper, Leo, Tom, and Eleanor nodded.

"That's why there were two notes in the eye window. *Confess* and *eight*. One was part of the game and one wasn't," Henry said as it fell into place for us all.

"All night long, you've been playing two games. One all in fun and another meant to harm you, I'm afraid," Eleanor said with a regretful grimace. "We've been trying to save you, but without access to the motherboard controller, we didn't have a way to do very much."

"But how did you cut off the power just now, then? Or was that Tyler, too?" I asked.

"No, that was all of us," Piper said proudly. "With Tyler downstairs and not monitoring the cameras, I only needed to distract Etta for a second. We knew they had to be looking for us, so we made some noise down the hall, from inside the wall, and when she came to find out what it was, Tom went through the passage in that room and cut the power."

"Luckily, we always keep a few pairs of night-vision goggles around," Eleanor said. "For late-night games of hide-and-seek." She giggled.

Tom nodded. "We had to act quickly—"

"But not quickly enough..." someone sang from behind us. We turned at the sound, a block of ice sliding down my spine as we spied Tyler and Etta standing in the doorway of the tunnel we'd just come from.

Tyler chuckled smugly. "Did you forget the cameras have playback, old man? As soon as you exited the secret passage to shut off the camera, we found your little hide-away." He clicked his tongue. "Sucks, 'cause, I'll be the first to admit, it *was* a really great plan."

"Just let the kids go, Tyler," Tom pleaded.

"*Shut up.*" He narrowed his cruel gaze. "Anyway, since we were so rudely interrupted, let me get back to answering questions. Let's see...where were we?" He pulled a gun from his pocket, pointing it at the group of us, bouncing from one to the next. "Ah, I remember."

I put my hands over my face instinctively, as Tom, Henry, Leo, and Shane stepped in front of us. I put myself in front of Eleanor. She trembled beside me, tears beading in her eyes.

"Ah, so brave. Not to worry, my friends, you'll all get your turn."

"Tyler, son, you don't want to do this," Tom said, shaking his head. He took a step toward him, his hand outstretched.

"Oh, but I really do." Tyler pointed the gun at Tom. "And I said *shut up.*" He fired without hesitation, and Tom crumpled to the ground.

"No!" Eleanor bolted away from me and to the ground next to her husband. Her hands were stained crimson as she tried and failed to stop the blood pooling out of his stomach. Without thinking, I shot forward, holding my hands on top of hers on the wound.

Eleanor shook with sobs. "No, please no."

"*Get back up!*" Tyler shouted. I didn't look back, too afraid to see if the gun was pointed at me.

"What did you do? He's going to die!" Henry yelled, moving once again to place himself between Tyler and me. "You can't want that. He's your uncle. This is between us.

This isn't about him. Let them go. Let them all go. This is between you and me. I made them do it. I made them help me. They didn't want to. They wanted to go to the police. It was me." He patted his chest. "It was all me."

"Very noble," Tyler sneered. "Do you think that makes it all okay? Do you think we should all hold hands and hug now? Skip merrily into the sunset? You didn't force them to do anything, Henry. They were all big girls and boys. They made their own choices. Now, they have to suffer the consequences."

"Come on, man, put it down," Shane said. "There's only two of you, and there's still a lot of us. You shoot again and you'd better hope you can kill us—"

He shot and Shane crumpled. I winced, my entire body jumping at the sound. Piper and Bethany rushed to his side, and I tried to see where he'd been shot from where I was. It looked like his shoulder. Through our husbands' legs, Bethany met my eyes, nodding once. I nodded back.

We'll get through this. Together. Like we always have.

Now, Henry stayed blocking my side of the room, while Leo had moved to block Shane, Bethany, and Piper. It was now or never. I reached up to touch Henry's hand once, my bloody fingers intertwining with his.

"I love you," I whispered.

He squeezed my hand tighter. The next few moments happened in a blur. Henry and Leo charged forward, launching themselves at Tyler. The gun rang out. Etta screamed.

I could hear the men struggling to keep him down, to get the gun away from him. When I glanced over my shoulder,

Henry had blood on his shirt, but I couldn't tell whose blood it was.

"Keep pressure here," I told Eleanor. She looked so frail and helpless sitting there, the thought of her life without Tom completely evident in her eyes.

I wanted to tell her so many things—how sorry I was, how I'd do anything to fix this—but there wasn't time.

I locked eyes with her once before standing up and rushing toward the pile of people on the ground. Just as I reached them, I saw the gun. I saw Tyler's face, his bloody grin.

"No!" Henry shouted, trying to shove his hand away, but it was too late. I flinched as the shot rang out. I covered my ears, collapsing onto the ground with the force of it. My insides were white hot with fire, like someone had taken a fire poker to my core. Every inch of me screamed for relief, and it was only then I realized I was screaming, too. I looked down, watching the blue of my dress stain dark purple. I placed my hands over the wound in what felt like slow motion.

"*Lakynn! No!*" Bethany rushed toward me, her cries unbearable as she tried to stanch the bleeding. It only made it hurt worse. I wanted to tell her to stop, but I couldn't say anything. I couldn't breathe.

Everything hurt.

Everything burned.

And yet, everything was numb.

I blinked, my vision growing fuzzy.

Eleanor was gone.

Blink.

Still gone. Had she been shot, too?

Blink.

Leo was on top of Tyler.

Blink.

Tyler was on top of Leo.

Blink.

Bethany's face was in mine. Her hot tears dripped onto my skin.

Blink.

Where was Etta?

Blink.

Where was Piper?

Blink.

Where was Henry?

Blink.

Who would take care of my kids?

Blink.

Would they hate me for what I did?

Blink.

What did I do?

Blink.

Calm.

Blink.

Calm.

Blink.

A voice floated over me, one I didn't recognize anymore. "Lakynn? Can you hear me? Stay with me, please. Stay with me. Please."

Blink.

Another voice. "Baby, can you hear me? No! Please, please stay with me. Please."

Blink.

A blaring siren.

Blink.

Peace.

Blink.

Why would I stay when I can go?

Where will I go?

There seemed to be no choice in the matter. I was floating.

Floating.

No more blinks. Only darkness.

Peace.

Falling.

Falling.

Floating.

The pain was gone.

I was gone.

Death is fast.

CHAPTER THIRTY-ONE

BETHANY

Two Days Later

When her eyes fluttered, a finger stirring at her side, I stood, moving to pace at the end of the bed. It was the third time she'd done that since we arrived. The third time in the two days since she'd made it to the hospital that I'd been given hope she was going to wake up, only to be let down when she didn't.

I chewed my thumbnail, watching closely for any other signs of consciousness as her breathing slowed again, her eyelashes going still.

The door to her room opened and Piper stepped inside.

"How is she?" she asked, her voice hoarse.

"Still here," I said, my chin trembling as I fought back tears.

She nodded, her expression grim. She ran a hand through her unwashed hair.

"How are you?"

She leaned her head to the side. "Still here."

Tears spilled over my eyes, down my cheeks. "She has to be okay."

"She will be," she said, chewing her lips and fighting back tears of her own. "We need her."

I sniffled, drying my eyes with the blanket I had wrapped around me. "Is Shane awake yet?"

"He was for a while."

I waited.

"Lizzie's with him now. I don't think he'll want anything to do with me after this." She shrugged one shoulder, brushing away a stray tear. "Not that I blame him."

"I wouldn't be so sure," I said softly. "Even after everything he heard, everything we confessed, I've never seen him look so happy as he did when he saw you in those tunnels. He cares about you."

She gave a solemn nod but didn't say anything else. She was afraid to let herself believe it, I knew, but it was the truth.

"I'm sorry about everything I said in the house," I told her, my voice low. "I was scared, and—"

"I know," she said with a quick nod. "I'm sorry, too. I never really thought you or Leo could be behind this."

"I know," I reassured her. "We're good."

"Tom's going to be okay," she said after a pause. "I wasn't sure if you got a chance to talk to Eleanor."

"I haven't, no. Not since yesterday."

I glanced out the window, where two bees buzzed lazily around the pane. Didn't they know the world was ending in here?

"His surgery went well. He'll be here for a few weeks, probably, but they're expecting him to make it."

I shook my head, wiping my tears as quickly as they fell. "How are we supposed to go on knowing this is all our fault? Leo was right. It's...it's too much."

She moved toward me then, wrapping an arm around my shoulder. "We go on because we have to. Because we have people counting on us. People who need us. We have each other. We don't get to go on for ourselves, not after what we did, but we have to go on to make life better for everyone who needs us." She shrugged, kissing my cheek. "It's as simple and as complicated as that." When she released me, she locked her pinkie with mine briefly, then released it.

The door opened again and Henry took in the sight of us, two cups of coffee in his hand.

"Anything?" he asked.

I shook my head, nodding in her direction. "She just moved a bit, but nothing substantial."

"I'm going to go back and check on Shane. See if Lizzie needs anything," Piper said, patting my shoulder. She wrapped Henry in a hug on her way out the door, breaking away just as she began to sob.

With the door shut behind her, he held the cup out to me, but I shook my head. I couldn't bring myself to eat or drink until my best friend was awake.

I didn't deserve to.

He sighed, sinking into a seat and placing the extra cup down. He touched her foot gently, running a finger over it. "The doctors say this is normal. She lost a lot of blood."

"Piper said Tom's going to be okay. He made it through surgery."

He took a sip of coffee. "I'm glad."

"Why isn't she waking up, Henry?" I chewed my lip, pacing again. "I've gone over and over it in my head. She was shot in practically the same place as Tom. He bled for longer. He's older. And yet, he's awake and doing just fine, and she won't even open her eyes." My voice broke and I covered my mouth with my hand, trying not to break down again.

"She's going to be okay, Beth—"

"How can you say that? *You don't know—*"

"Because she has to be," he said, standing up to face me. He didn't dare touch me. "She has to, okay?"

I sniffled, pulling the blanket around my shoulders farther.

"You're tired. You should go home and rest. I'll stay with her for a while."

"I'm not leaving her side until she's awake."

"You've been awake for three days straight. Don't you want to go check on Leo? On your kids?"

"They're fine. They're not in a hospital," I snapped.

He sat back down, accepting there was no point arguing with me, and I returned to pacing.

"She's probably just—"

"Do you think we deserve this? Is this because of us?"

His jaw went slack, and he stared at me, brows drawn down. "*What?*"

"Is this... Are we to blame for this? We lied to her. We're the reason Tyler came back anyway. If we'd just let him go that night he'd—"

"You can't think like that," he said, standing up. He moved toward me, but I stepped back.

His hands went up in surrender.

"Why can't I?"

"Because..." He paused, and when he spoke again, his voice cracked and tears glistened in his eyes. "Because if this were our fault, it should be us in that bed, not her. She doesn't deserve this."

"But this hurts so much worse," I sobbed, clutching my chest. "I wish it was us."

He reached for me, and this time I didn't shy away. I fell into his arms, and we held each other up as we broke down, crying for all that we'd lost and all that we stood to lose.

For so long, I'd avoided any private moments with him, for regret over what we'd done and fear that it might happen again, but there, in his arms, I knew it never would. Our hug was simply a moment between friends. That was it. The insignificant moments we'd spent together all those years ago were nothing compared to the years we'd spent as friends, raising families next door to each other, waving in the carpool lane, grilling out next to each others' pools.

I'd spent my life running from the past, from the moments I thought defined me, but what if I was wrong? What if the years and years of moments where I'd made good choices, where I'd raised a beautiful family, built a perfect life, and loved my best friends wholeheartedly, could someday outweigh the one terrible mistake I'd made?

Was that how it worked?

I wasn't sure.

And I didn't know if I'd ever be sure.

What I knew was that we'd get through this together, like we always had. We'd wait for Lakynn to wake—because she would, she had to—and we'd help her to get better every step of the way.

We'd tell her about Eleanor's moment of bravery that saved us all. How she escaped the room through the tunnels during all the commotion and hit a panic button that signaled for the police. How Etta had gone after her, but it was too late. Eleanor managed to outsmart her in the tunnels.

We'd tell her how everyone survived and how the four of us had told the police everything, confessed and tried to make it right. For the first time in our lives, we didn't have to keep the secret anymore. We'd get to tell her that we were free. Since Tyler wasn't actually dead, and after all that had happened—all the evidence they'd found in Tom and Eleanor's home—the police had assured us they had a much larger case to deal with and weren't interested in pursuing charges against us.

We'd tell her that our bad moments truly don't define us forever and sometimes there is beauty in letting things go. Even if you spend your life making amends for the bad. Even if you never quite forgive yourself.

It's okay to give yourself grace.

"She's going to make it," I told him, giving a sharp nod as we broke apart, sniffling and wiping our eyes. He nodded, and I could see similar thoughts in Henry's eyes, too. It was the culmination of everything Tom had said in the tunnels and everything Piper had said just moments ago.

We were the sum of all our choices, good and bad. Maybe other people wouldn't see it that way, but we had to believe it ourselves if we ever hoped to live with what we'd done.

In some strange way, I was thankful for what had happened.

It taught us so much.

It freed us.

It made us stronger.

Like always, something that should've torn us apart, brought us together. And we were better together, I had to believe that.

"She's going to make it," he repeated, nodding slowly.

"We all are," I promised him, and when I turned to face her bed, her fingers stirred, her eyes fluttering open, and my own eyes blurred with tears. It was true. "We all are."

ENJOYED THE DINNER GUESTS?

If you enjoyed this story, please consider leaving me a quick review. It doesn't have to be long—just a few words will do. Who knows? Your review might be the thing that encourages a future reader to take a chance on my work!
To leave a review, please visit:
mybook.to/thedinnerguests

Let everyone know how much you loved
The Dinner Guests on Goodreads:
https://bit.ly/3tUg5fI

DON'T MISS THE NEXT RELEASE
FROM KIERSTEN MODGLIN

Thank you so much for reading this story. I'd love to invite you to sign up for my mailing list and text alerts so we can be sure you don't miss my next release.

Sign up for my mailing list here:
kierstenmodglinauthor.com/nlsignup

Sign up for my text alerts here:
kierstenmodglinauthor.com/textalerts

ACKNOWLEDGMENTS

First and foremost, to my incredible husband and wonderful little girl—thank you for allowing me to chase my dreams. Thank you for loving me, believing in me, bragging on me, traveling with me, and cheering me on every step of the way. None of this would mean anything if I didn't get to share it with the two of you. I love you.

To my bestie, Emerald O'Brien—thank you being the person I turn to for everything. Thank you for asking the hard questions, pushing me to be and do better, always being willing to listen to me vent, and being my biggest cheerleader. I'm so lucky to call you my best friend, my Michael and my Maya, and to share that amazing moon with you. Love you, friend.

To my immensely talented editor, Sarah West—thank you for making sure my stories are the best they can be. I'm so grateful for your guidance, insights, questions, advice, and encouragement.

To the proofreading team at My Brother's Editor—thank you for being the final set of eyes on my stories before they go out into the world. It's always scary to release one of my literary babies, but with you guys on my team, I worry a lot less. Thank you for polishing my novels until they shine!

To my loyal readers (AKA the #KMod Squad)—thank

you for everything! For the excitement over each new book, the reviews, the recommendations, the shoutouts on social media, the gifted books to your friends and family, the TikToks and bookstagram posts, the Facebook love, and so much more. I've had thirty-two books to thank you for all you've done for me and it still isn't close to enough. Without you, I'm just a girl with a head full of stories and no one to share them with. Thank you for believing in me.

To my book club—Sara, both Erins, June, Heather, Dee, and Rhonda—thank you for being a highlight of my week, for always being excited about my news (big or small), and for reminding me how much books can change lives. I'm so thankful my stories brought us together and I'll forever be grateful for your friendship.

Last but certainly not least, to you—thank you for purchasing this book and supporting my art. I've always dreamed that someday someone would hold a book with my name on it, crack it open, and discover a world entirely of my own creation. With this purchase, you made my dream come true. I'm so very grateful for you. Whether this is your first KMod book or your 32nd, I hope it was everything you hoped for and nothing like you expected.

ABOUT THE AUTHOR

KIERSTEN MODGLIN is an Amazon Top 30 bestselling author of psychological thrillers, a member of International Thriller Writers, Novelists, Inc., and the Alliance of Independent Authors. Kiersten is a KDP Select All-Star, a recipient of ThrillerFix's Best Psychological Thriller Award and *Suspense Magazine*'s Best Book of 2021 Award. Kiersten grew up in rural western Kentucky with dreams of someday publishing a book or two. With more than thirty books published to date, Kiersten now lives in Nashville, Tennessee with her husband, daughter, and their two Boston Terriers: Cedric and Georgie. She is best known for her unpredictable psychological suspense. Kiersten's work is currently being translated into multiple languages and readers across the world refer to her as 'The Queen of Twists.' A Netflix addict, Shonda Rhimes superfan, psychology fanatic, and *indoor* enthusiast, Kiersten enjoys rainy days spent with her nose in a book.

Sign up for Kiersten's newsletter here:
kierstenmodglinauthor.com/nlsignup

Sign up for text alerts from Kiersten here:
kierstenmodglinauthor.com/textalerts

kierstenmodglinauthor.com
www.facebook.com/kierstenmodglinauthor
www.facebook.com/groups/kmodsquad
www.twitter.com/kmodglinauthor
www.instagram.com/kierstenmodglinauthor
www.tiktok.com/@kierstenmodglinauthor
www.goodreads.com/kierstenmodglinauthor
www.bookbub.com/authors/kiersten-modglin
www.amazon.com/author/kierstenmodglin

ALSO BY KIERSTEN MODGLIN

<u>STANDALONE NOVELS</u>

Becoming Mrs. Abbott

The List

The Missing Piece

Playing Jenna

The Beginning After

The Better Choice

The Good Neighbors

The Lucky Ones

I Said Yes

The Mother-in-Law

The Dream Job

The Liar's Wife

My Husband's Secret

The Perfect Getaway

The Roommate

The Missing

Just Married

Our Little Secret

Widow Falls

Missing Daughter

The Reunion

Tell Me the Truth

ARRANGEMENT NOVELS

The Arrangement (Book 1)

The Amendment (Book 2)

THE MESSES SERIES

The Cleaner (The Messes, #1)

The Healer (The Messes, #2)

The Liar (The Messes, #3)

The Prisoner (The Messes, #4)

NOVELLAS

The Long Route: A Lover's Landing Novella

The Stranger in the Woods: A Crimson Falls Novella

THE LOCKE INDUSTRIES SERIES

The Nanny's Secret